MONSTROUS LONGING

Abi Hynes

First published 2023 by Dahlia Publishing Ltd
108 Spencefield Lane Leicester LE5 6HF
ISBN 9781913624125

Some of the stories in this collection have appeared elsewhere, in a slightly different form:

Little Brass Lamp in *minor literature[s]*, The Something in *Deracine Magazine*, Long distance (stars and stars) in *Neon Magazine*, Phantasmagoria in *Black Static*, The Pure of Heart in *Syntax & Salt*, The Welcoming in *Lucent Dreaming*, Customer Reviews for Ashley Wiccan's Wonder Lust Love Potion in *BFS Horizons magazine*, The Mark in *Interzone*, Rosie in *Splice Press*, A Conversation Recorded Before the End of the Experiment in *Splice Press*, Lady Macbeth in *Litro*, The Gastrosophist in *Boudicca Press*, Silt *in The Molotov Cocktail*, Ready or Not by Fairlight Books, and The Savage Chapel' in *The Short Story*.

A CIP catalogue record for this book is available from The British Library

For Rachel

Contents

Little Brass Lamp   1

The Something   4

Long distance (stars and stars)   13

Phantasmagoria   18

The Pure of Heart   33

Monstrous Longing   36

The Welcoming   54

Customer Reviews for Ashley Wiccan's
Wonder Lust Love Potion   60

Mr Thornton's Mother   67

The Mark   71

Rosie   86

Lady Macbeth   91

The Gastrosophist   93

Silt   97

Her Outer Self   99

Ready or Not   113

A Conversation Recorded Before the   119
End of the Experiment

The Savage Chapel   138

Acknowledgements

About the author

Little Brass Lamp

When my husband came home, there was something different about him.

His long service was over at last, and I had spread the kitchen table with all his favourite foods, and set the incense burning, and beaten the rug until the dust rose from it like magic smoke. And sure enough, on the thirteenth hour of the thirteenth day of the thirteenth year he'd been away, a little brass lamp appeared beside the thali. The lamp was scuffed and dented and ordinary. I held it between my legs and rubbed, and he slipped into my lap like butter.

'Hullo, wife,' he said, and kissed me.

He ate ravenously. He was smaller than I remembered, but perhaps he'd just got larger in my mind. His hair, which had been short, snaked down his spine in a long, dark plait. He had changed so much that I might not have known him if it hadn't been for the birthmark, just visible above the collar of his shirt.

He helped me clear away the dishes, and he held my hands beneath the surface of the water. I felt the bones of his fingers against mine, light as little goby fish. His skin was smooth where it had once been calloused. I remembered the old roughness of his touch with a sudden flush of heat, like the rush of hot air into a cool house when you open the door to the street outside. We lay in bed that night like strangers and watched the lamplight dance on the ceiling through the net above us, my own skin tingling.

We found a gentle way of life together. His newness troubled me, and at night I dreamed of chasing him through crowds of people, calling his name, the back of his head bobbing in and out of sight. But he brought home tulips, and planted vegetables in the garden that he cooked for me himself. He had been gone so long that I had to tell him stories of our old life together. And, in return, he told me of his travels, and of the people whose hands his little lamp had passed through.

'What did they wish for?' I asked him.

'The wrong things. Wealth. Power. Sex.'

'Did it make them happy?'

'Sometimes,' he told me, his black eyes sparkling. 'But only by accident.'

'And what did you wish for, when they set you free?'

He smiled and wouldn't tell me.

One day, he came home with a long, thin instrument. He pressed the reed against the swell of his lips, and out from the bell of it came tumbling sounds I never thought a man could make. It sounded a note in me, somewhere deep behind my stomach. A long, low note that murmured through me like I were a singing bowl; like he had struck me, here, just so.

That night, we lay where we fell. His birthmark rubbed away under my kisses and stained my lips; a deep, secret red. We matched the rhythm of our breathing, slow and musical, as I lay against the softness of his breasts. I let my fingertips follow the silver spider-lines on the curves of his hips and thighs, thinking many things that I might have asked him about the strangeness of his body. But we had come this far; it would have been awkward to bring it up.

Don't get me wrong. I still loved my first husband. I

2

hoped that he was happy somewhere, and if it was with another woman, I wouldn't have begrudged it. We can't always help whose laps we fall into.

I sealed the lamp, and now I keep it on my windowsill. Sometimes I think it rattles, but I'm sure it's just the wind.

The Something

It's hard for Andrea to pinpoint the exact moment she became aware of the Something in her house. It had always had a sort of personality, squat little new build that it is. Its roots spread deeper than is immediately obvious from outside. Its kitchen delves into the ground in a bizarrely old-fashioned design that leaves its little windows peeping just above the front lawn, offering an ankle-only view of passers-by to whoever does the washing up.

Other aspects of its layout seem to defy logic and good sense. The two first floor bedrooms connect with each other, corridor-style. You have to pass through the ensuite to reach either of them, rendering the guest room… Well. Bloody inappropriate for guests.

The house asserted its own character with a pleasing confidence. It was one of the reasons Andrea had bought it. (An impulsive purchase, a Fuck it, why shouldn't I? Giving off that dizzy rush of power. I am master of my own destiny!) Quickly, the house felt like a companion. It was co-conspirator in her emancipation from sharing unsatisfying flats with unsatisfying friends. She liked the Something, especially coming home on quiet, dark nights. The house's confidence was catching.

The Something started small. It was the towel she noticed first (though there might have been other things before. Andrea could be dreamy. Unobservant.). Clean and dry and folded neatly on a now-closed toilet lid. It was an unambiguous gesture, as there was no question of Andrea having put it there herself. Her towels were never folded,

4

never carried in preparation to the bathroom. Her journey, dripping and shivering, to the airing cupboard in the guest bedroom, and then back, was part of her morning routine.

As a gesture, it didn't frighten her. Her house wasn't like old houses. It didn't groan and whistle and scrape when the wind got up. It only sat there, resolutely silent, its burglar alarm and double-glazing primed against intruders, all its corners clean and cheerful. The Something was not a grisly intruder, Andrea was sure. It was just… the house itself.

And it was a helpful Something. The kitchen bulb blew one evening, leaving the almost-cellar too dark for chopping onions. It turned out well; Andrea called a friend, they had too much wine with dinner, she found herself staring at his hands. And when she scrunched her way downstairs next morning, the bulb burned bright and good as new.

The Something, she began to realise, had its preferences. It liked it when they watched telly together (batteries in the remote – changed by the time she got home from work) and when she ate at home (salad – fresh – it had definitely been on the turn). It liked it less when she brought her spreadsheets back with her (a sudden leak from the en-suite, targeting her laptop bag), or when she sat up late trawling Facebook, her thoughts emptying into that little blue screen (three iPhone chargers, so far – fried themselves in power sockets that were harmless when it came to bedside lamps.) She felt, in some irrational part of herself, that it rewarded her for good behaviour, and punished her when she pissed it off.

When a week of miserable weather and a bad Friday meeting sent her crashing headfirst into an early night with

5

her kindle, a mug of tea stood waiting for her, still steaming, on the bedside table. Utterly unapologetic about its own existence. When Umar called her (that was his name – the brown-eyed school friend – Umar) on a Sunday morning, stayed for lunch, stayed, there wasn't a single fucking fork to be found in her kitchen (or anywhere at all – she checked) for forty-eight hours.

She told her sister about that one little exasperating chapter. (She didn't quite spell out her suspicions. How would she phrase that: I think my house is jealous?) and Lois laughed with her, enjoying the hand-me-down annoyance.

'You've got a poltergeist.'

When the Something left its first message, Andrea could hardly say she was surprised. She had been late for work. Her alarm hadn't gone off, and when she'd scrabbled about for her phone to check the time, it wasn't by her bed. Five minutes of searching didn't reveal it; not down behind her bedside table, not somehow underneath the mattress, not forgotten in her coat pocket when she crept down to check. The clock in the kitchen read quarter past nine.

She flung herself back up the stairs and tugged on her least-creased suit, unshowered and already clammy with panic. Without her phone, she couldn't check her meetings, but this would be her third late appearance this month. Mornings had been a struggle lately, though she had always been an early riser. She was delighting in sleep in a way she never had before, not even as a teenager, and in her freshly painted bedroom she was sleeping longer, better, deeper. She gave up on her phone and pelted back into the kitchen for her car keys.

Her mobile was there. It was sitting exactly in the middle of the kitchen table where she couldn't have left it, where it couldn't have been five minutes ago. On top of it, covering most of the screen, was one of Andrea's own pink post-it notes. It read:

Sick Day.

X

It seemed so casual. It was written in biro and the handwriting was unfamiliar but ordinary; a little childish, perhaps, with the way the letters neatly joined together. It was the sort of note a partner leaves, to remind you that it's bin day. The shape of the 'X' (a kiss? Really?) was relaxed, but definite. It was absolutely impossible to find the note alarming.

Andrea called in sick and sat down at her kitchen table in her work clothes. Her meetings didn't seem to matter now. All her anxiety about the office faded as soon as she hung up the phone. Her late-waking grogginess cleared, and the day was hers. The anticipation of it was blissful.

She made herself a huge, extravagant breakfast: spicy eggs and toast with jam and coffee and orange juice. She ate it slowly with sunshine pouring in through the kitchen window and pooling at her feet. She thought of walking up to buy a paper, a real one, just for the aesthetic, but she was too content, really, to brave the outside world, and the idea didn't linger. It seemed like a gift to her, this day. She felt as though the house had given it to her.

That evening, she ignored the emails from work and the texts from friends and she slept naked for the first time in years. She spread out her limbs and let the heat of her body spill into the cool sheets. The house embraced her until she fell asleep.

In the days that followed, Andrea's grogginess returned. It was as if someone had dressed her in particularly heavy clothes; she felt slow, and bulky, and tired. Work was a strain. She was surrounded by loud, insensitive people, their mouths always moving. (Didn't they realise they were talking too loud and too close?) She cringed away from them. She'd started grinding her teeth, which gave her headaches in the afternoons, to the point where the shrill jangling of her phone or a fire alarm test would send her, shaking, to the toilets, head between her knees for a while and slow, deep breaths.

'You're not yourself at the moment,' Dani scolded her, when Andrea had refused another invitation for a post-work drink. 'We never see you. What's happened?'

Andrea buttoned her coat up to her chin, wishing she could go on buttoning, up and up over the top of her head and right down to the toes of her boots.

'I'm a bit worn out this week,' she said. 'I just really want to get home.'

The Something was angry when she was late. After a train cancellation and two replacement buses, Andrea longing for her front door the whole way, she crossed the threshold with a gasp like a drowning creature surfacing, to find the house was freezing cold. It was almost spring, and the air inside was icier than it had been in the street; a nasty, immovable sort of cold that seeped up through the soles of her feet and stung her fingers. It made no sense. Except she knew the game by now.

The boiler was in the bathroom. Andrea went to investigate, praying for a pilot light, hopeful that the Something might forgive her and set things straight now she was home. But she didn't get that far. The door to the bathroom was jammed tight shut (frozen? Did doors do that?), and no amount of teasing the door handle or barging it with her shoulder or kicking it would persuade it to budge. Andrea felt weak and tearful and pathetic.

'Please,' she murmured to the bathroom door, too upset to feel ridiculous. 'I'm sorry.'

The house was silent. She wanted to go to bed, to draw the covers up over her head and sleep this away, but her bedroom, both bedrooms, lay beyond the sealed bathroom, at the end of the strange upstairs corridor that was now completely inaccessible.

She stood on the landing, her breath misting out in front of her, and for a moment she considered knocking on her neighbour's door. What would the house do, confronted with a stranger? Would it be brazen enough to defy logic and sense like this in the presence of a witness? But she didn't know her neighbours. She had never made the effort to introduce herself, she had been happy as she was. And how angry would the Something be with her afterwards, when they were left alone again?

She went back downstairs. She was desperate for a wee after her long journey home, and there was nothing for it but to squat in the garden, trousers around her ankles, eyes watchful for cars returning to nearby driveways. She slept on the sofa in her suit under several layers of coats, and dreamed that someone was crouching beside her in the darkness, their breath on her cheek a welcome source of warmth.

When Andrea woke the next morning, she was very ill. She was sweating and sore, but at least when she threw off her makeshift covers, the house was warm again. Her head swam as she made her way, trembling, up the stairs, where the bathroom door stood innocently ajar. She bent to run herself a bath, and stripped off to reveal skin that was pale and puffy. She sat on the toilet, knees hugged to her chest like a little girl, and saw the second pink note, stuck to the mirror opposite, already bubbling with the steam.

Curfew. 7pm.
X

It was the same careful handwriting, the 'X' precise and unhurried. It served as both a symbol of affection and a signature; it asserted itself as a message from someone who knew Andrea intimately enough not to sign their name. She coughed, and the sides of her throat sawed at each other. She lowered her aching body into the hot water and let it soothe her.

She was miserable and feverish all weekend. Umar had been calling, but she felt lazy and revolting, and wanted to be left alone. He left three messages, each less hopeful than the last. The final one asked her to meet him after work on Tuesday, and she might have accepted (she'd be feeling better by then, wouldn't she?), but by the time she crossed the city it would be 6:30, at least. She turned her phone on silent, and he didn't call again.

Things went along peacefully for several weeks. Andrea forced herself to get up earlier so that she could be in the office by 8am and catch the 5.16 train home. She just couldn't seem to fully recover from her bout of flu; her headaches were back with a residual, sinister sort of force that made everything feel a bit too far away. She dropped out of her own social life in favour of rest and quiet. The thought of being energetic and interesting exhausted her, and she felt a shiver of relief every time she crossed the threshold of her own home, back into its welcoming arms, back amongst its familiar, musty smell that she breathed in with a sigh, like a lover's scent. The Something was always pleased to see her. She put off her sister, who was always threatening to come and stay, partly out of fear that they might be discovered.

'I'm fine, Lois. I'll come and see you soon. I'm just working really hard at the moment – you'd be bored.'

She lay back on the sofa, and masturbated to nothing in particular, her own smell mingling with the smell of the house, her toes stretching upwards into emptiness, and she imagined she felt someone brush them lightly; the offhand gesture of someone who loves you passing by.

She started to wish for the next note. The Something was teasing her. It took to hovering outside her bedroom, its figure almost visible through the crack in the door, but always gone when she opened it. She burned with restlessness when she went days without hearing its whisper beneath the whooshing of the dishwasher, or the gentle bumping of its fingertips against her calves when she

11

climbed the stairs.

But when the final note came, the wait was worth it. Lying on her pillow, in the imprint of her head still warm with sleep, it gave her just one word:

Tonight.

X

At the kitchen table, cradled by the dark, Andrea keeps her breathing quiet and shallow. A few moments ago, she thought she had heard footsteps behind her, imagined the feet of strangers passing level with her head where the street met the kitchen window, completely unaware of the tension they were interrupting in the squat little house. Probably, they thought it was like their own ordinary new builds, housing-by-numbers, all standard measurements. Whoever had built Andrea's house had been an architect of a different kind.

Far away, in some upstairs corner of the house, she is certain she hears something take a breath.

Long Distance (stars and stars)

Sam

I wake up suddenly cos she's sitting on my chest. Her knees are by my ears and, well, she's naked – I mean she's totally perfectly naked so that is quite a sight. And you'd think it would be sexy wouldn't you and I mean it is, it definitely is sexy, it's just that actually it's also quite intimidating, waking up to find a fully grown naked woman sitting on your chest at 3.15am when you haven't been expecting it.

Not that I'm ungrateful. It had always been a bit of a long shot, growing her from scratch in that Petri dish like we had to cos it's so much cheaper, and frankly the guy we got the stuff from looked dodgy as, so the fact that she turned out a woman at all and not some sort of fungus was pretty great and thanks very much and all that. It just took me by surprise is all. The chest-sitting.

I cover her up cos it's the proper thing to do. The clothes Louise left for her are there hanging all stiffly in the wardrobe but it doesn't seem right somehow, launching into all that straight away. I put her in one of my old t-shirts and she looks perfect in it like a little girl, so pure, so newly minted. She looks like Louise but not like Louise at all. Her hair is almost the right colour, but brighter, like I've never seen red before. I want to kiss her right then and there but well – you've still got to be a gentleman, haven't you?

When we Skype, Louise shows me her Sam substitute. Bless her, he hasn't turned out so well. He is more or less man-shaped I suppose and his hair in the strange patches where it does grow is dark like mine. He's about a third of the height he should be – maybe the atmosphere interfered with his incubation? – so he looks like a potato with arms and legs. She gets him to wave at the webcam and I can see his fingers are webbed. He seems friendly and happy enough but really, how could we tell? He doesn't even have a mouth.

'How did yours turn out?' Louise asks me.

'Still waiting,' I say, not ready to share her yet. 'Maybe tomorrow.'

'Fingers crossed,' she says. Potato Sam tries to cross his fingers, but he can't because of the webbing.

I can't put it off forever so a few days later I introduce them. Louise looks a bit miffed to tell you the truth – but then she would do, seeing as hers turned out such a dud.

'What are you going to call her?' she asks. It's the first time we've talked about it. We knew the long distance thing would be hard, but then there are all these surprises that we weren't prepared for. The 'Louise substitute' we'd said until now, when she'd only been an idea and not a living breathing person with her blue-white skin and her expressive hands and her eyes that look so trusting or quizzical at me through their not-quite-human shade of blue. We decide on Louise.2, as in, 'Louise.2 learned how to make your banana pancakes yesterday.' But when it's just the two of us, I call her Lou. As in, 'Lou, I'm not hungry, come back to bed.' I'm supposed to teach her how to be like Louise but I can't bring myself to do it. I teach her how to dress herself but I don't teach her how to tie her shoes.

I set her up so she can use my Spotify account while I'm

14

at work. I never did that with the real Louise cos she was scoffy about my music taste and anyway she only listens to podcasts. But Lou only listens to the playlists I set up for her. It's brilliant seeing her face light up when she hears a song she likes, and we listen to our favourites together on lazy Sunday mornings, me muttering the lyrics to her, Elvis Presley, Johnny Cash. Sometimes we turn it up loud and dance together like it's our own private party and she's like a baby in my arms she's so perfect and I call her that – 'Baby' – and I can't stop looking at her. Blank and bright and perfect, perfect.

Louise.2

I'm learning all the rules and I am very good at them. The rules are Don't go outside without Sam and I must wear clothes. Eat the food he makes for dinner and not the raw chicken and the TV has a button that is on and the shower has a handle to twist and that is on as well and no singing when Sam is sleeping because he has work tomorrow. Shoes are for going somewhere and slippers are for staying. Sex is for a quiet happy and dancing is loud happy and crying isn't happy and you stroke his head and say 'There there' and the kettle is for hot water and the freezer is for cold. Learning is good but not too fast when he is looking and always point at things and sometimes say 'dog' when you mean 'car' and 'boom' when you mean something he can't understand. 'A+' means very good and when he says 'Lulu' sometimes he means me.

He is teaching me some of his language. The words he

teaches me are mostly about himself: he points at things and says 'suit', 'briefcase', 'razor', 'Sam'. 'Saaaaaaaam,' I say and he claps in delight. I like the way he thinks the things in front of him are so important they should all have their own words. He is obsessed with the fact that he is male and this body he made for me is not. 'Me man', he says, pointing at bits of himself. 'You, woman.' He is always cheerful after that.

He talks to a woman on a little screen. She is very far away, he says. On another planet – it will be years before she can come home and they will both be old then. She has a funny blob man with her who always wears a tie, and they talk to each other in sign language. She loves him but Sam doesn't notice. He says she is doing special work learning about the universe. He is proud when he says this and it hurts me in my chest but he believes it. They go to other worlds and they look at the ground and they say 'This is a rock' and they are very pleased with themselves. 'Rock,' I say back to him, and watch him smile. 'R-ock.'

We go for walks in the park and I bring him things I think he'll like. Interestingly shaped pebbles and rainbow coloured plastic and a piece of bone a dog has chewed and he says 'Would you look at that' like they are very precious. When it's cold, he wraps me in his coat so we are like one person and I think all the thoughts for both of us while he looks happily at the sky.

When the time comes for me to go, I think I'll take him with me. He will be frightened but I will hold him close and tell him stories that are as true as he can manage. I like to listen to his heartbeat when he sleeps; it is like a little drum, so certain of its own existence. 'Tomorrow, tomorrow, tomorrow,' it says. So sweet and steady in its little lie. Little drum, little perfect drum. He has been lonely, but now I am here and he won't be lonely anymore.

I will explain some things to him but I will keep some of his mistakes because they are nice and funny and it is too lovely to listen to the way his mind works – the odd, illogical leaps it makes. He thinks there are lots of rules and bad things will happen if he breaks them. He thinks the woman on the screen is coming back. He has a drink that makes him sad, and then he says, 'Our love has travelled light years. Between us there are stars and stars.'

Phantasmagoria

***Phantasmagoria**: a sequence of real or imaginary images like those seen in a dream.*

We spent half an hour trying to 'thread the needle'. You sit on the floor, plant one foot and lift the other. You clasp your hands, and as you try to stand (one-legged, remember, like a heron) you *thread the needle* of your lifted leg through the eye of your arms. Then back down again, each movement in reverse. It was the sort of torture-disguised-as-training that our physical theatre teacher enjoyed. She liked to demonstrate, at length, and then watch us fail, marking against our names on her clipboard when we did. I had the sort of swollen, second-year-of-uni body you see worn by girls who didn't go to private school and are spending their own money for the first time: on beer and chips to fill the space inside them which has recently become huge and lonely. It was a body that had always wanted to move, but it had been through enough high school PE lessons and village hall ballet classes to know that it would only be punished for it.

Our university's music and drama building had been two blocks, once. At some point during modernisation they had been joined together but the floors didn't quite match up, which meant bizarrely sloping corridors and a fourth floor which, without the aid of a lift or a staircase, became the fifth, but only if you walked the length of it from one direction. There was a studio there that I could only sometimes find, with mirrored walls and a sprung floor that the suited classical musicians and the heavily made-up drama queens of my cohort had little use for. Usually, the blacks were drawn across the mirrors to make the windowless, low-ceilinged space feel even darker and more airless, so that standing alone in it meant trying to breathe as though with a hand over your mouth.

Phantasmagorical: *having the appearance of an optical illusion, especially one produced by a magic lantern. Changing or shifting, as a scene made up of many elements.*

The physical theatre teacher's name was Cassie. She had a severe haircut that should have been comic, but wasn't, and she was particularly fond of teaching us about what she called 'the cruelty of clowning'. She liked to get us up on stage, one at a time, in silence and with no instructions, to an audience of our classmates who were told to raise their hands as soon as they were bored. *This is nothing,* she would tell us, if we looked hurt or angry. *If you'd gone to drama school, you'd have to do this every day.* In warmups, she would get us to stand in a circle, arms windmilling, chanting, 'I've been to Lecoq!', which she had, but only for one summer. In our second class with her, we had to take turns to be dogs on leashes, while she gave us points on her clipboard for barking at birds, sniffing each other's arses, and pissing up against trees. At that point, one red-haired girl I'd always thought was rather sour walked out and didn't come back. I had a newfound respect for her after that.

Because most people had forgotten it existed, I found that I could block-book Studio 5 for most of the semester.

I drew back the heavy black curtains to reveal the mirrors and wrestled two chairs from the complicated jungle of stage scaffolding behind the jammed partition. I found some heavy blue gym mats against the wall and laid them out to practice forward and backward rolls, always heaving them upright again before I left in case the cleaners complained. I guessed and strained my way through a series of half-remembered stretches I'd never have attempted if anyone else could have witnessed them. There were only three bands that I loved, and their songs reminded me of home too painfully, so though I often brought speakers and a laptop with me and set my girlfriend's iTunes on shuffle, it was more of a nuisance than an inspiration. And all the time I watched myself in those mirrors in a way I never had before. I watched like Cassie watched – like I was a stranger in the audience who didn't know myself.

Phantasmagoria (also fantasmagorie, fantasmagoria) was a form of horror theatre that (among other techniques) used magic lanterns to project frightening images such as skeletons, demons and ghosts onto walls, smoke, or semi-transparent screens. In many shows, the use of spooky decoration, total darkness, (auto-)suggestive verbal presentation, and sound effects were also key elements. Some shows added all kinds of sensory stimulation, including smells and electric shocks. Even required fasting, fatigue (late shows) and drugs have been cited as methods of making sure spectators would be more convinced by what they saw.

I knew I'd never be a dancer (I'd left it too late, I was too

20

fat, I'd never have been fit enough), but I still wanted to be an actor, so I auditioned for the Drama Society plays in my first year at university. The older students liked to put you off while you waited in the corridor to be called, telling you how the director was dating one of their housemates, or recounting horror stories of past auditions when they'd had to play single cell organisms gradually evolving, and were encouraged to writhe on the floor and 'mate' with each other. I spent one particularly gruelling afternoon repeating a monologue by a second-year about putting a teabag inside my knickers, playing opposite a line-up of increasingly Dorito-flavoured boys because the other girls going for the role had been at a party the night before and were too hungover to show up. I didn't get that part; the writer had *wanted* to give it to me, she assured me, but the director had already promised it to one of her hungover friends (the director had been at the same party, and hadn't turned up to my audition, either).

Phantasmagoria *is a point-and-click adventure horror video game designed by Roberta Williams for MS-DOS and Microsoft Windows and released by Sierra On-Line on 24 August, 1995. It was made at the peak of popularity for interactive movie games and features live-action actors and footage, both during cinematic scenes and within the three-dimensionally rendered environments of the game itself. It was noted for its violence and sexual content.*

Three years after *Phantasmagoria* came out, and only two years after my family bought a home computer, my little sister and I discovered the multi-disk game on one of our parents' bookshelves. I was nine, and Susi was six. On investigation, we were told it was an 18 and inappropriate for children. So we played it secretly.

In the game, successful mystery novelist Adrienne Delaney and her photographer husband Don Gordon have just purchased a remote mansion previously owned by a famous 19th-century magician, Zoltan 'Carno' Carnovasch, whose five wives all died mysteriously. Adrienne, who had hoped to find inspiration for her next novel in her new home, starts having graphic nightmares as soon as they move in, and is comforted by the loving and supportive Don.

While exploring the grounds, Adrienne finds a secret chapel hidden behind a bricked-up fireplace. She opens a locked box that lies in waiting on the altar, and accidentally releases the evil demon that forced Carno to murder his wives. The demon possesses Don, who starts acting menacingly towards Adrienne, and rapes her.

Through a series of visions, Adrienne learns the various gruesome ways in which Carno slaughtered his spouses. Hortencia, who avoided his abuse by secluding herself in her greenhouse, is stabbed with gardening tools and suffocated with mulch. Alcoholic Victoria gets into an argument with Carno, who impales her with a wine bottle through the eye. An overly talkative third wife, Leonora, has her mouth gagged and her neck twisted 360 degrees by a torture device. And the food-loving Regina is force-fed animal entrails through a funnel until she chokes to death.

Reading the synopsis on Wikipedia, I find I can replay each of these scenes clearly in my mind. Once you reached each point of discovery, the game would trigger a three-minute video that couldn't be stopped, paused, or skipped once it had started. Susi and I could, of course, have left the room, but that option never seemed to occur to us.

The Wikipedia synopsis states that the story ends when Adrienne successfully expels the demon from her husband, and escapes from its resulting fury long enough to perform a ritual that traps it once again inside the hidden chapel. I have no memory of that ending, because Susi and I never won the game. The ending I remember is round after round of being chased through the house by the still-possessed Don, who kills Adrienne in a different way depending on which room he catches her in: the greenhouse (a trowel of dirt forced down her convulsing throat), the hallways (wine bottle through the bursting eye), the kitchen (glistening animal entrails, the practical shape of that funnel). The end we dreaded most of all came if he caught her in the chapel itself, trying uselessly to click on items that might let us perform the exorcism. Here, he would strap her into a chair disguised as a conjurer's machine and turn the handle that brought a guillotine-like blade down sideways through the centre of her skull, splitting it open and showing us the meat inside.

I have searched online, but I can't find a description of this ending anywhere.

***Étienne-Gaspard 'Robertson' Robert**, the most famous phantasmagoria showman – a Belgian inventor and physicist from Liège. He would often eliminate all sources of light during his shows in order to cast the audience into total darkness for*

23

several minutes at a time. Robertson would also lock the doors to the theatre so that no audience member could exit the show once it had started.

Robertson sited his entertainment in the abandoned cloisters kitchen of a Capuchin convent (which he decorated to resemble a subterranean chapel) near the Place Vendôme. One of his first phantasmagoria shows displayed a lightning-filled sky with both ghosts and skeletons receding and approaching the audience. To add to the horrors he projected onto smoke and screens, Robertson and his assistants would sometimes create voices for the phantoms. Often, the audience forgot that these were tricks and were completely terrified. In fact, many people were so convinced of the reality of his shows that police temporarily halted the proceedings, believing that Robertson had the power to bring Louis XVI back to life.

When I spotted a callout for an independent production, advertised as a physical theatre project of the kind that nobody in the straight-laced Drama Society usually went anywhere near, I couldn't resist. The director, who we'll call Matthew (he's a literary manager at a major theatre now, according to LinkedIn), was a third-year with plans to start his own theatre company, named for the length of time it took him to travel from his parents' London house to his university accommodation. I liked Ella, his producer, more than I liked him, but his avant-garde tastes and his 'not-fitting-in-the-boxness' spoke to me. The show was his own adaptation of *The Yellow Wallpaper*, and he and Ella had persuaded Manchester Museum to agree to let them stage it in some of their unused attics.

I don't remember what I did in the audition, but I was unreasonably thrilled when Matthew called to tell me he was casting me as 'the woman in the wallpaper': a part that, admittedly, had no lines, but did require a physical performance that sounded pleasingly glamorous.

The Yellow Wallpaper *is a gothic short story by American writer Charlotte Perkins Gilman, first published in January 1892. A young woman and her physician husband rent an old mansion for the summer. To help her recover from her 'hysterical tendencies' after the birth of their first baby, he confines her to the nursery and forbids her to read or work. During her imprisonment, she imagines she sees a woman trapped within the room's yellow wallpaper, with whom she eventually trades places, or goes mad, depending on your point of view.*

You know what's coming. The reality was not quite what I'd pictured when I'd gleefully accepted the role. This was first heralded by Lola – a girl on most of my courses who regularly got drunk and told me I was beautiful so effusively that it made me suspicious of her motives. She sat down next to me at the start of our Theatres of the Middle East seminar and announced that she had been cast in the play she knew we'd both auditioned for: as the woman in the wallpaper.

It turned out there were three of us. I tried not to let the fact that I was sharing the role knock the shine off it too much, and in fact Lola, Hannah and I became friends. In rehearsals, we were united in our resentment towards the much posher and (in our view) significantly less talented

25

India, who had all the lines and who Matthew had started referring to as his 'muse'. We, meanwhile, wriggled and writhed on against the walls on cue, occasionally adding in some spooky whispering, stopping only to be corrected by Matthew if he caught our octopus arms tiring and straying too close to the floor. ('It's the yellow *wallpaper*, ladies, not the yellow carpet!')

It had been made clear to us from the offset that our costumes were going to take the form of yellow leotards. When we were presented with them they turned out to be made entirely of transparent, stretchy lace, and the shawls and gowns we had been told we would wear over them had been scrapped because Matthew didn't think they looked right. We were in the basement of his student house, which had been chosen for this pre-production costume fitting and photoshoot because of its appropriate grimness. The three of us stripped off, and I tried to brazen my way through the embarrassment of my childish bright purple underwear while Ella fiddled with the lamps and Matthew's camera clicked. We all laughed at how dodgy this would be – a director luring us to his basement to take photos of us barely clothed – if Matthew weren't gay. Ella's laugh was a little strained, I thought, but perhaps I've misremembered that.

At the time, my primary worry was that I was the largest of the three wallpaper women, and I sucked my stomach in so tightly during the costume fitting that I ached afterwards. Looking back at photos now, of course, I was lovely in the ordinary way that all 19-year-olds are lovely; soft, with rounded edges and a bad fringe that made me look even

26

younger than I was. There was no talent or skill in my performance. Matthew wasn't interested in choreographing anything but the basic blocking that affected India, so we made up our wiggles afresh every night, and often missed our cues. But the overall effect, I'm told, was good – we were stationed behind gauze screens that hid us from the audience until the back lights blazed, and we could travel through and amongst them in the dark. And there had been a few points during rehearsals when it had seemed we might be onto something, when the excitement of discovery that was in the mind but also in the body had me tingling from head to foot. We were working on the end sequence, when the women burst out of the wallpaper at last and helped India to hang her husband, and the ideas were flowing freely between us. We tried a solution, which presented a new idea, which gave way to another, and I put forward a suggestion for the final moments of the show that we all knew was right. Perhaps I'd gone too far, though, because Matthew looked me straight in the eye.

'Do *you* want to direct the play?', he asked me, and I shut my mouth.

The best thing about that part in *The Yellow Wallpaper* by far was the shedding of some of my self-consciousness in that bizarre, revealing costume. In the last days of dress rehearsals, up in the museum attics, we three lace-clad women drifted about the building like yellow-stained ghosts. We took photos of each other in various contorted positions, marvelling at our creepy/sexy limbs, all tangled up together. Matthew had mostly lost interest in what we looked like, so we undertook various unsanctioned makeup

27

tests, settling on a gold shimmer that we rubbed all over our arms and faces. We ate our lunch on the staircase, not caring how many baffled curators walked past.

The Theatre of Cruelty *(Théâtre de la Cruauté) is a form of theatre generally associated with Antonin Artaud. It has been described as a break from traditional Western theatre and a means by which artists assault the senses of the audience. Artaud's works have been highly influential on artists including Jean Genet and Peter Brook.*

Artaud wanted to abolish the stage and auditorium, and to do away with sets and props and masks. He envisioned the performance space as an empty room with the audience seated on the centre and the actors performing all around them. The stage effects included overwhelming sounds and bright lights in order to stun the audience's sensibilities and completely immerse them in the theatrical experience. Artaud believed that he could erode and audience's resistance by using these methods, 'addressed first of all to the senses rather than the mind'.

In our last ever class with Cassie, she put us into pairs. I worked with Asha, one of the only two brown-skinned girls on my course, and we were instructed to observe and then mimic each other: first standing, then walking. Cassie split the group in half, so that I sat in the stalls and watched as Asha did her Abi-walk around and around the stage, weaving in between the other mimicking students – all trying to be careful, still, at that point. Trying not to hurt anybody's feelings.

'Bigger!' Cassie called to them. 'Show me everything ten

28

times bigger!'

Asha winced. She leaned back slightly and pushed her stomach – my stomach – forward. My face felt very hot, and I could smell the bitter tang of fear rising underneath my t-shirt. Cassie hovered at the edge of the performance space, her expression eager. *This is nothing! If you'd gone to drama school...*

'*Bigger!*' she shouted, walking amongst the students now, marking her clipboard with her hard, staccato ticks. 'Come *on* now, I want to see it from space!'

Asha let her stomach yawn forwards like a pregnancy. She waddled, pigeon-toed, and swung her arms vigorously, mannishly, at her sides. She tucked her chin so that the skin of her neck gathered in rolls, her crotch leading her back and forth and back and forth. There was no laughter in the room as I remember it. The performances were grotesque, obscene, completely ridiculous by the time that Cassie was satisfied with them, but those of us watching also knew that they were true. Most of us left the workshop that afternoon in silence, and when I got back to our flat I got straight into the shower, where I hated every inch of my own flesh so violently it felt like a promise, or a spell. I stayed there for a long time, and my skin burned and burned with shame.

In his lifetime, Artaud only produced one play that put the theories of the Theatre of Cruelty into practice. He staged and directed Leo Cenci, adapted from the dramatic work of the same title by Percy Bysshe Shelley, in 1935 at the Théâtre des Folles-Wagram in Paris. The play was neither a commercial or critical success and ran for only 17 performances.

The Yellow Wallpaper was the first and the only play that I was cast in at university. Too afraid of humiliation to keep auditioning, my girlfriend and I started producing our own shows, which I acted in at first but then, realising I was often the least talented performer in the room, soon stopped. We raided the drama department's costume store, a musty-smelling warren full of clothes donated by various local theatres, in which all the women's clothes were tiny and the men's were huge, like the way characters are drawn in Disney films or superhero comics. I abandoned my body to do as little as it wanted, and tried instead directing, and then writing. I was homesick for a home that had vanished when I left it; I was hungry and empty all the time, and never satisfied. If a bad photo sent me spiralling into self-hatred and despair, I would spend a few weeks starving myself and swimming lengths between lectures, or drag myself to ballet classes at the Dance House that made me feel like an idiot for ever imagining that I could move, let alone that anyone might like to watch me.

But I continued to choreograph dances and movement sequences for our little company's productions, and often only for myself, returning to Studio 5 to work for long hours alone right up until I graduated. I scribbled them down in notebooks in my own form of clumsy dance notation, but mostly I relied on the memory of my body, which clung to whatever felt good and seemed to tell the truth of something inside me that couldn't find expression any other way. Where Cassie's classes had punished me for showing up, my private hours in Studio 5 were nourishing in a way that I couldn't have explained to anyone. The scenes I created there were wordless, and often violent. I presented back to myself the shapes that women's bodies made in the films and plays I studied, and the shapes I had seen them make long before I arrived at university. The results were naïve and earnest and troubling. I'd had no formal training beyond what we did with Cassie and it showed. I had thought that getting a degree and studying the thing I wanted to do would be enough, but of course it wasn't. It took several tutors over several years (for I invited them to my plays even after I'd left) to hint, gently and not so gently, that I was kidding myself before the message really sunk in. I let the creature I had spied in the mirrors behind those black studio curtains (who was cruel as often as she was kind, who was me and not me) drift into the past tense. When she returned to me in the dark – distorted, improbable, phantasmagorical – I blinked until she faded into the walls.

Theory: *every story about a woman's body is a horror story.*

In our final year, I saw Lola in a production of *Les Enfants Terribles*, co-directed by Hannah and another friend of ours. She was excellent in it, much better than the girl who won 'best actress' at the student theatre festival awards that year. But she gave up acting altogether, then – a self-flagellating move I understood completely. Another friend I did my Master's with went off to drama school after we graduated the way I'd always planned to – and sent back horror stories worse than anything Cassie had inflicted on us. A few years

31

ago, Cassie's husband died suddenly, leaving her and her two young daughters devastated – I saw it on Facebook. These days we have some mutual friends, and I've seen her sometimes, at the bar before a show or waiting to pitch for the same small pots of local arts funding. I've changed her name in case she ever reads this and recognises herself, and thinks I've been unkind.

I have seen my own ghost many times since university. She still visits; I see her face beneath my face, her sharp teeth inside my mouth. She likes to surprise me in the bathroom at house parties; she can move where she likes, you see, insubstantial as she is, projected onto smoke. She presents herself, maimed and rotting, in my nightmares. Sometimes, for months, or even years at a time, I will be afraid to look at photographs of myself, knowing that she'll appear in half of them – disguising nothing, revealing me to everyone.

The Pure of Heart

You are fifteen, and you are wearing your tightest dress. You're dancing with a guy who is probably called Mike. You don't actually know if that's his name because the pop music is so loud the sticky floor is vibrating, but he made a 'Mike'ish kind of shape with his mouth when he said it.

Probably Mike is your responsibility now, because your friend is getting off with his friend and those are basically the rules. He's bought you a Bacardi and coke—the only drink you know how to order—and even though it's gross, when he asks you if it's your favourite drink, you say 'Yes.' But you're regretting that, because now he thinks you're the sort of person who's, like, *really into* Bacardi and coke and that does not feel like a true reflection of your personality.

Probably Mike is twenty-one. Kissing him feels like having your face licked by a big dog, so you're trying to do it as little as possible.

You keep him talking. Probably Mike likes films and games with dragons in them. He's a bit of a sci-fi and fantasy nerd, he says. You know he does not mean this in the way that you mean it. You know this because he is wearing a big silver chain and very white trainers. He says he thinks you would look great in a gold bikini. You suspect you are not going to be able to talk about *A Wizard of Earthsea*.

You say you're going to the toilet. Probably Mike says he'll buy you another Bacardi and coke when you come back, and winks. You try to find an escape route. You find a door behind a curtain that leads through to another room.

33

In this room, everything is quiet.

You suddenly feel very heavy. The room is empty except for one chair. In the chair sits an old woman.

Between you rests the worst thing that you will ever do. It is in the form of a great dark rock. Its cracks and creases are your future lifelines; they are your reasons, your excuses, your apologies. They tell the story of your future self.

This old woman's eyes gleam huge behind her glasses. Behind her waits a little rowing boat on a green ocean, which is strange, because you live in Preston, and you're fifteen and you're in a nightclub and really none of these things should be here at all. But if you want to take the little boat, if you want to float away from Probably Mike and the next Bacardi and coke, then you will have to take the rock with you. It is too heavy for the little boat.

The old woman asks if you are pure of heart. You don't know what that means. She runs her fingers over the rock, over the worst thing that you will ever do. She bows her head and lets it murmur in her ear. She nods.

She says that you must break the rock by promising to be very, very good for the rest of your life, so that the worst thing you will ever do will never happen. You promise to be very, very good for the rest of your life.

'That doesn't work,' she says. 'You have to mean it.'

It's getting difficult for you to think clearly. You don't understand why you feel so heavy. You reach into your pocket and you realize it is full of little stones.

The little stones are like the big dark rock; they are all the bad things that you will do from now until you die.

You look at the old woman, who is waiting patiently. The

worst thing you will ever do is huge and jagged. You look at the water, where sail the pure of heart. You look back at the door, which leads to Probably Mike, to the rat-a-tat-boom of the club music, to your parents who think you are staying at a friend's house.

You take your bad deeds out of your pocket, one by one. You drop them into the water. Its green skin ripples and splits with your tiny splashes.

The day you'll lie to save yourself.

The times you'll be too frightened to be good.

The way you'll make yourself a martyr.

How often you'll betray the things you know.

The time you'll cheat, and win.

The ocean fills. The old woman looks at you, her lips pursed. She looks at the great dark rock, the worst thing that you will ever do, which waits there, heavy and unharmed. There is a path now through the water, paved with all your wicked deeds, which lie in wait for you.

You do not sail where sail the pure of heart. You walk.

Monstrous Longing

Figure 1: Rumour.

Christina, Queen of Sweden. You might have seen the paintings; heard, perhaps, that somebody wrote an opera. Probable lesbian, possible hermaphrodite. Almost certainly a hunchback with a coarse mouth and no patience, who abdicated her throne at the age of twenty-eight to avoid marriage and convert to Catholicism.

If you've heard none of these things, it doesn't really matter. The marquis, Giovanni Monaldeschi, had heard them all, and he still followed her to France. You could say, what happened to him next was all his own fault.

Later, when the horrified dignitaries of France and Rome had stopped clutching their pearls and the gossip was handed over to the artists of Europe, people said that Christina and this marquis were lovers, and that his fate was a crime of passion. You can see the appeal of this story. Jealousy is something that the French can understand. A woman might, if she were driven to it, kill for love. Even a noblewoman might spill the blood of her paramour across the polished floors of a gallery like a baker floods the golden casing of a tart with sweet, crimson jam.

Christina was furious when she heard this rumour. For one thing, she did not consider herself a woman, and therefore refused to be condemned for such a female crime. She was a prince. She was a lion like her father. She wrote later: To attack me is to attack the sun.

36

Figure 2: Ice.

Christina was born in the middle of the Little Ice Age, in the coldest winter Europe had known for a thousand years. The sea froze. The ice on the rivers throughout Sweden was so thick, the peasants took to lighting fires on them which could burn for days. Her father, leaving the palace for the first time since his daughter's birth, was stopped in his tracks by a bird dropping from the sky in mid-flight, frozen to sudden death.

They might have said it was a bad omen. But you do not say that to a king.

When Christina was born, she was so dark and hairy and covered by caul they thought she was a boy. They told the king as much, and let him spend thirty pleasant minutes imagining the celebrations on the streets of Stockholm. But meanwhile, in that savoury-smelling birthing chamber where his wife lay panting, the mistake was being discovered. And the unlucky doctor and the queen's women were panicking over what to do about it.

'Could we rear her as a prince?' the midwife asked.

'The child does have a lusty roar,' agreed the king's doctor. 'Suggestive of a masculine spirit.'

'And all that hair!'

'But what happens when the truth gets out?' asked a serving woman, who still had birthing blood all down her apron.

'We could be far away by then,' said the midwife. She had a sister in Uppsala and had been saving up to visit her. 'Let some other servants deal with it.'

37

In the end, it was only the child's aunt Katherine who put a stop to these schemes and dared to tell her brother of the error. She took the baby to the king, naked despite that terrible winter, to take a look himself.

'I am content,' said Christina's father. 'She will be clever, for she has deceived us all.'

Her parents called her Christina; the same name as her dead sister, who had been the only other of their children to have been born alive. Not even a name of her own, which might tell you something of what the king and queen thought her chances were. Still, the second Christina grew, and the story of her birth became a legend on the streets of Stockholm, with the bit about the frozen bird falling out of the sky told quietly so as not to count as treason.

Figure 3: Naples.

There has been nothing to do all autumn at the Palace of Fontainebleau, where the great men of Rome have tried to hide her away. She was causing too much trouble to stay in Italy so they plumped for France, where they tell her to go hunting. Octobers here are not the frozen ones of home; the forest that surrounds the Palace has caught fire with amber and orange and deep red. If she weren't so preoccupied, she would have liked to gallop through the golden hues of those trees. Murderous sword swinging; blood scenting the air.

I could have been a great warrior,' she tells anyone who will listen, 'if were not troubled by an excess of compassion.' She was known for pinching and kicking palace servants she didn't like. Most of her maids had little purple splotches up their arms.

The Cardinal who invited her here is a man of many promises. To Christina, he has promised the throne of Naples. He tells her that the Neapolitans long for their emancipation from the Spanish.

'And then who better to rule them than you?' he asks, his damp hands clasping hers. 'A queen without a country. A ruler of experience and wisdom. They will be so grateful; they will kiss your boots.'

The ache for power has been growing in her, a seedling at first, but now a tree with its roots deep inside her body. She has never been to Naples, but what does that matter? She has Monaldeschi, a Neapolitan of her very own, to complete her education.

Monaldeschi is a tall and energetic sort of man. He has hazel eyes beneath very dark eyebrows, and one of those faces which, half-hidden by his beard, might have been any age between twenty and forty. Women like him because he is noisy and he laughs easily and he moves like a man who expects everybody to get out of his way; because women seem to like these tendencies, he has never learned to curb them. Christina likes him enough to make him her Master of Horse.

'You are my only friend, Monaldeschi,' she tells him. 'You are my true friend, aren't you?'

They spend the summer in France, living far too quietly for someone who loves perpetual action and excitement. He spends his days following the Cardinal's instruction to flatter and distract this little Swedish tyrant. So Monaldeschi drinks with her and obeys her whims to sit up talking long into the night. Philosophy, religion, art, love – it is all the same to Christina. She likes an argument, likes to feel she's bested him, and over and over he bows or winks and tells her, 'You have me there, Your Majesty'. For the first time in his life, he learns to shrink himself, and to lower his voice for the comfort of someone else. He brings her little treats and watches her pick fishbones from her teeth. He lets her see his gaze linger on her body as though he wants her, but the truth is that he cannot admire her, cannot desire her, does not want her as his queen any more than he wants a pitchfork up his arse.

Christina is restless. Once promised something, she is a child again; who does the Cardinal think she is, to make her wait for anything? There are no women there to teach her patience. Until now, she has surrounded herself by men, and she has never questioned whether it ought to have been otherwise. She wishes she had not cropped her hair so short; she would like someone to brush it and braid it. There is nothing so comforting, and Christina – though she would rather be tortured than admit to it – is much in need of comforting.

Figure 4: Women.

The doctor and the queen's women were wrong if they thought Christina's father wouldn't love her. That, as it turned out, would be her mother's role. She kept away from her daughter, who in her absence came to share the popular opinion at court that her mother was an idiot. The lion had chosen badly there: Maria Eleanora was a German countess, and she was very pretty but also, according to almost everybody, very stupid. The lion was lucky to have bred with her at all because he was away so often, partly because he was fighting the long war but also because he didn't like her very much.

For the first six and a half years of her life, Christina saw the queen only occasionally. When she did, she was repulsed. At this young age, Christina had an overwhelming aversion to everything that women did. She couldn't bear their fussy clothes or their heavy perfumes or their gossiping. She could never be made to wear a hat or a mask, and though she would consent in winter to be dressed in gloves, the servants of the royal castle would find them mischievously stuck onto statues or hurled into fireplaces, and her small hands numb and almost blue with cold.

It was around this time that Christina became aware that she was a hunchback. Although, truth be told, it was only quite a little hump, and once noticed she reassured herself that it did not undermine her dignity in the slightest. At six years old, she believed that it was the reason that Maria Eleonora didn't love her. But she developed a special way of walking, which she found was easiest in flat shoes, and prided herself on her ability to disguise the fact that she had one shoulder slightly higher than the other.

'Really,' she likes to tell her friends – she tells Monaldeschi, over and over – 'there are people who have met me many times and cannot tell at all.'

It's true that she learned to ride a horse so well and lightly that any man watching from a distance took her for a little lord, and would not guess that she was riding side-saddle, all

41

her small might poured into that one gripping leg so that she didn't tumble off and destroy the reputation she was already building as the sharpest, the most fearless, the least feminine of royal daughters in all of Europe since her idol Elizabeth I of England. She loved learning and took to languages particularly well. Under her aunt Katherine's care, she began the training of a future ruler, and played the part of the prince so well that the kingdom gave up wishing for another.

Figure 5: Letters.

It's a maid who tells Christina that Monaldeschi has betrayed her. She is just some serving girl – with thick hands and sleeves spotted with kitchen grease – but she presses something into her hand as though she's not afraid to touch her. It is a letter wrapped in wire, but the wire has been cut. The Cardinal, to Monaldeschi, thanking him for his service. He writes: She will not have Naples.

Christina clutches her stomach as though she has lost a child. She is suddenly overwhelmed by an intense longing for home; for the first time in years, she yearns for the cold, and for the familiar tastes of pickled herring and sticky-sweet cinnamon buns. She wants to be held, even by this dirty servant child, and she holds out her arms but then remembers her dignity and pushes her away. After all this long dull summer while she grew fat on French pastries and the marquis flirted with her, after all the Cardinal's reassurances. After all that the Cardinal writes that Naples will have no emancipation after all, because the European tug of war has ended and between France and Spain there is suddenly talk of peace.

Peace! She hates the word. Her nickname is 'Pallas Athena': the goddess of war. She is a lion like her father. She wants to rule a kingdom again and if she cannot have the one she gave up then she will make men bleed until she has another.

The Cardinal has been playing all sides in a rigged game that only he can win. Naples did not matter to him after all: he had promised it to her, to the Duc de Guise, to protect it for the Spanish.

Over the weeks that follow, more letters wrapped in wire come and go from Fontainebleau. Christina's men are waiting. They tear them from the hands of the Cardinal's messengers, who are quickly silenced along dark corridors. Christina copies them herself. Each letter she shapes hurts and fuels her in equal measure.

In approximately twelve minutes, Monaldeschi will start pleading for his life. He doesn't know this yet, but the animal part of him senses it coming; he is tense in his bed, unable to sleep, his nose reading traces of intent on the night air.

'I am your devoted subject,' he had told her, all that summer. 'Naples will love you just as I do.'

Figure 6: Love.

When Christina was seven years old, her mother came to claim her. Gustav the lion had been brought, broken and lifeless, from his battlefield, and she refused to let them bury him. She took their daughter from her tutors, who had

43

found her temper difficult and her sense of self-importance almost impossible, but Christina was nonetheless devastated to be torn from her French and Latin, her daily studies of algebra and astrology and music.

Her mother also prised her from her aunt. If she had not been such a little princeling, she might have clung to her skirts and screamed that day. She did beg just a little for Katherine to refuse her mother, but the whole kingdom was afraid of the fierceness of the queen's grief, and Maria Eleonora, who had never loved her daughter for her cleverness or her boisterousness, who had seen only her crooked back and her lack of all things weak and soft and feminine, had clasped her close at last. Her husband was dead and she wanted Christina, his daughter and the last remaining piece of him on earth, all to herself.

Christina was given her own rooms in her mother's house, but she was never allowed to sleep in them. Maria Eleonora had the child brought to her that very first night and made her kneel beside her as she said her prayers, which she said in German. Christina could have spoken them with her well enough, but even then she had begun to take pleasure in murmuring her own prayers in Latin. And besides, she was angry with her, so she bowed her head but kept her lips pressed very tight together.

She tried very hard not to look at her mother. Whenever she did, she saw again the image of her bending low over her father's body, which no longer looked like her father and had already begun to stink, kissing and crooning over his dead, grey face, tenderly combing her fingers through his hair, weeping so hard her tears pooled in the crevices on the waxy surface of his face, murmuring to him, between her bouts of weeping, like they were lovers still.

'May I go back to my rooms now, Mother?' Christina would ask her, when she finally rose up from her damp amens.

'No, daughter,' she said, her voice still wet and grating. 'You will share my bed with me. You are the only comfort left to me and I have great need of you.'

It would not be quite accurate to say that Christina was the last remaining piece of Sweden's king in the earthly realm. The queen was not content with delaying her husband's burial for three long years, and returning as often as she could to kiss and caress and cradle his once-great head in her arms. After a distasteful length of time, even for a Swede, and long after that first brutal winter that had kept the ground too hard had passed, she finally allowed him to be interred. But she bargained, even then. She would allow them to take his body only if she could keep back the most vital part of the man she had loved so madly and unrequitedly.

She made her demand at a time when the court and its politicians (soon to be Christina's court, and Christina's politicians) were so embarrassed by her protracted, uncivilised grieving, so despairing at the great scandal of their noble lord remaining unburied for so long, that they agreed. And so above that bed that she now commanded her daughter to share with her, preserved in an ornate jar whose beauty could not belie its gristly contents, lay Gustav's heart. Those who came to know Christina later could tell you that she had an iron stomach, how she was

45

never seen to flinch from gore or swoon as ladies do, or turn her face from sights that set other people's guts churning. But then she was at an age when the imagination is at its most sensitive; when ghosts and devils and all manner of mysterious and spiritual horrors seem capable of wrapping themselves up in the merest shadow. As she climbed into bed beside the dowager queen that night, and every night they shared together after, Christina's limbs shook so violently that her mother had to pinch her to make her lie still. She lay awake for hours, sweating beneath the layers of furs her mother needed to keep the Swedish chill from her frail bones, listening to her own frantic heartbeat. Certain that beneath it, quiet but steady in its reproachful drumming, she could hear her own dead father's.

Beside her, Maria Eleonora was restless too. Her dreams were fitful, and she often clutched at the child, as though she were the babe in need of comforting and not the other way around. Or else Christina would feel a yearning, lustful heat rising from her, and then her limbs would come creeping, and her stroking and petting could only be stopped if she thrashed her legs violently enough to wake her. Sometimes, her mother would retreat abruptly to her own side of the bed, perhaps in shame, perhaps only in anguish at discovering the small child's body where she wished her husband's to be. There were times, too, when she would cling to her daughter on waking, her sour breath drifting over my face, murmuring that Christina was her darling and that she loved her, and begging her to say she loved her in return. But Christina would not say it, however long she kept it up. So, the widowed queen would weep all the harder, sometimes long into the night. Christina put my fingers in my ears.

But those were not the worst nights. The very worst were when Christina did sleep soundly, or else she lay so still and breathed so deeply that Maria Eleonora thought she did. For then, in the madness of the midnight hours, her mother would take down the jar of liquid and meat and she would hold it to her, whispering obscenities to it, covering it with kisses, pressing it against her breast and Christina never knew what else, for after the first time she woke and saw her at this she always kept her eyes shut.

When morning came, the jar was always back in its place. Maria Eleonora was happiest in the mornings, and she would sit and have Christina brush her hair, while her ladies would check the sheets for spots of her blood that came less and less frequently. She would never marry again. All of Europe knew that she was mad, and that the only child she would ever bear detested her.

Figure 7: Night.
Christina's guards drag Giovanni from his bed and brought to the Galerie de Cerfs – the gallery of the deer. That is precisely what he looks like, she decides. He is all big brown eyes, wide as though in innocence or disbelief. If he had no trousers on, she'd be able to see his twitching tail. That makes her laugh, and for a moment the men in the room – her guards, of course, and the old prior she has summoned none too gently from his bed – look at her as if she's mad. But then they remember themselves.

47

She stands here now, on this night the others think is cold, wrapped in a sable coat that stifles her. She is regal despite her diminutive height, her hunched back only detectable when she moves, which she does now – pacing. Monaldeschi is surrounded by her armed guards who now block his exit.

She has also dragged the elderly prior from his bed to act as witness. Monaldeschi, she informs the prior, who is still picking crusts of sleep from the corners of his eyes, is on trial for treason. Nobody points out that you can't commit treason against a once-queen, or even a might-someday-again-be-queen. She brandishes the copied letters before Monaldeschi's astonished deer-eyes. He has to stoop for this; she is barely more than half his height. But he is not afraid yet, despite the cold. Despite the darkness of the Galerie de Cerfs, and the lamplight licking at the flanks of the painted animals to the left and right of him. He has never met a woman he could not charm. He doesn't think this one, with her stockinged legs and Swedish accent, will be the first.

'What have I done?' he asks her. 'Tell me, dearest queen, who has lied about me?'

'I trusted you,' she says. Like a line from a play. Deep inside her something is fluttering. Some little panicked creature, trying to escape what she is doing. 'You have betrayed me. You never meant me to have Naples. What have you to say?'

And so he talks. He explains, he reasons, he even humbles himself a little to the lady with the shorn hair who now stands in judgement of him. He speaks for two hours on his innocence. Christina's guards make shadow puppets for each other on the polished floor; the prior's knees and back pain him so badly that he chews the inside of his cheek to gristle.

'The prior here can verify that I gave you ample opportunity to defend yourself.' Christina is pleased with how untroubled her voice sounds. The prior manages a nod. He is thinking that he is so cold, his fingers feel like old leather. 'I have heard your suit, and now I sentence you to die.'

From beneath her sable she pulls the Cardinal's letters with a flourish: a gesture she has practised. And the marquis sees it now. The threat. The murder that is about to happen here. But much too late.

He falls to his knees.

'I beg you,' he says, completing the scene she had imagined. 'Spare me.'

She will not, but she likes to be asked.

Figure 8: Childhood.

At thirteen she began to govern Sweden. They admitted her to council meetings and she sat at the head of a long table flanked by men who mostly did not look at her, propped up on a cushion so that only the toes of her boots could touch the floor.

The meetings were long and tedious. But she didn't fidget, didn't allow herself to practise her Greek in her head or chew a hangnail. This same year, both her tutor and her aunt – the only people who had loved her – died and could not help her anymore.

Christina's grief manifested itself in bad dreams and an obsessive interest in religion. It was too much for her mother. Having finally put aside her mourning for her husband, Maria Eleonora found her daughter's pain was a burden she was ill-equipped to carry. Besides, the child was to belong to Sweden, just as Gustavus had belonged to that wretched frozen country, and Maria would not repeat her mistake of loving someone she would have to share.

And so Maria Eleonora moved to Denmark. Christina threw open the windows of her mother's rooms and ordered that they be aired for a full year, until the snow that blew in from the open windows threatened to melt and cause a flood, and a servant was brave enough to quietly close them. When Christina came of age and claimed her throne, they began to talk to her of marriage, and she remembered what it was to share a bed, and the monster of her mother when she was a wife no longer. She gave up her throne. She exiled herself from her own country, and looked instead for God's love among the Catholics.

She did not find it.

Figure 9: Mercy.

When Monaldeschi at last begins to plead, Christina has not been queen of anywhere for four years. It has been long enough to teach her that the life of a subject can never suit her. She is too wild, too loud, too large for every room she enters. They tell her she is masculine, and perhaps they mean the clothes she wears and her feathered hats; but really she thinks they mean the fact that she laughs without covering her mouth, and she never smiles coyly or casts her eyes down. Without her crown she is only an oddity, and nothing of her life so far has prepared her for it.

Monaldeschi starts to cry. It spoils his handsomeness and doesn't move her an inch; she is ready to give the order just to stop his snivelling. But then the old priest is beside her, and Monaldeschi's sweaty hand is on her arm. The priori is buzzing in her ear in French so fast that she can only catch one word in three, but she feels the meaning of it.

'Are you sure?' the impertinent fellow is asking her. 'On whose authority can you condemn and kill a man in France?'

Christina throws him off and looks down at the sobbing marquis. All those days, she is thinking. All those nights, I thought you loved me. And while I slept you wrote your letters, full of all the ways you did not love me at all.

'Your majesty,' he weeps. There are rivers of snot trickling through his beard, but even those she does not trust. Should she pardon him, to let him wipe his face and laugh at her?

He does seem sorry. He tells her all the things she needs to hear so badly. She is a true monarch, favoured by God, born to rule as Caesar ruled, anointed one, most blessed, most benevolent, admired by all. He knows her to be good and just and places himself entirely at her mercy.

She hesitates. She carries a sword, but she has never touched a man with it.

The marquis sees her bend. The prior sags and staggers. The rivers in Monaldeschi's beard stop flowing.

'I love my country,' he says to her. 'I would never have betrayed you, had it not been for my country. Spare me, and

51

I will tell all Naples of your goodness. My mother and father will kiss the ground you walk on if you spare their son.'

He says this to Christina, who has never been loved, who has never had a lover. He talks of love to someone who is so afraid of it, the word makes her feel sick. His country, he says, his parents, love, I love, they love me.

Figure 10: Fire.

She sends the prior from the room and leaves it herself. It takes the marquis fifteen minutes to die, which feels like a long time to him and to Christina's guards whose hands have gone so numb that they can barely grip their swords. Monaldeschi, although unarmed, is wearing a breastplate under his clothes. It's a precaution that turns out to do him no favours, for it takes a slice to the belly, blows to his face and head, the loss of three fingers and, at last, a dagger to the neck before the life spills out of him.

The guards and the prior go to their beds. In Sweden, where the hours of daylight have shrunk to a pale sliver, her cousin Charles who wears her crown now murmurs in his sleep. Christina's guards are too tired to wash themselves; they leave the marquis' blood staining their clothes and smudge the cooling gore across the mats they sleep on.

Christina is thinking already of what Europe will say about what she is done here. Whether there will be a reckoning. They cannot know, she thinks, they will not understand. If you have never been a queen, how could you comprehend how great a thing that is to lose? If you have only ever been a queen, how could you bear to be anything else?

She goes to Monaldeschi's room. A fire is already laid there and she lights it, crouching so close to the little crackling flames that if her hair were longer it would catch and burn. Instead, she feeds to it Cardinal's letters, watching as the wire glows and curls up, and the paper and ink turn to black dust.

The Welcoming

The woman who I suppose is my grandmother takes a long time to come to the door. I can see her moving about in the hallway, inching closer but taking her sweet time about it, stooping to do god knows what. The wobbly pane of glass in the door distorts her movements, so she looks like she's swaying.

I'm disappointed. I would have liked to come and see my father in a house that I knew, perhaps even had a key to. I would have liked to let myself in and surprise him in the kitchen, busy with whatever we would eat later, delighted to see me two hours earlier than expected, apologising for the mess but there not really being any.

The woman who is supposed to be my grandmother makes me feel like a giant when I step over her threshold. Everything in her house is small and low, and when she pulls me down to kiss me on both cheeks I have to bend almost in half. I feel flustered at this immediate, forceful affection. Her lips leave little cloying damp patches on my face, and I feel that I have done something wrong somehow; that there was a fault with the embrace and the fault was mine. I stand there for a moment feeling ashamed – too hot in my massive coat with my massive suitcase, staring at the chunks of mud I've already trampled into the pale green carpet with my massive boots. I look around for Dad.

'The bed's made up for you in the nursery, dear,' she says. 'Could you take your things upstairs?'

She expects me to know where I'm going, so I pretend I do. There is only one upstairs door ajar, and so I push that open and I put my suitcase and my coat and my boots in the neatest arrangement I can manage, just inside it.

The bed is a single one, and very narrow. It's made up the old-fashioned way with tightly tucked layers of blankets instead of a duvet – one corner turned down to expose the yellowing bedsheet – and an ancient hot water bottle, which is already lukewarm. I wait and listen for Dad's voice calling me or his footsteps bounding up the stairs but the house sounds like the end of a breath: the barest whisper of life left in it.

When I go back down, the woman who must be my grandmother is still waiting in the hallway. She doesn't look at me, but fiddles with a fussy little clock on a fussy little side table. She lifts it up and straightens the doily beneath it and sets it down again. I scan her face for anything familiar; a jaw like my sister's, or my aunt Emma's nose, or that shape of the eyes that make people say my dad and I are so alike sometimes. But her features are vague. It's like my mind can't fix on them. Like I'm forgetting what she looks like even while I'm looking at her.

'You'll be wanting your tea now,' she says to the fussy little clock. I look at it; it's just gone five pm. I had a late lunch on the train about an hour ago, but I follow her as she shuffles off towards the kitchen, trying and failing to say that I'm in no hurry, raising my voice down the dingy corridor for other ears. Only when we reach the cramped, linoleum-floored room, there's nobody there either.

'Is he still at work?' I ask her, but she doesn't seem to hear me. On the tiny kitchen table she has set one side plate, and on it is a piece of cold ham, one slice of bread and butter,

55

and two leaves of gem lettuce.

'Is this for me?'

'Oh yes,' she says.

There's only one dining chair. I squeeze myself into it, and she sits herself in an old, winged armchair in the corner to watch me.

'Aren't you having anything?' I ask.

'Eat up now,' she says. 'Your dad will want to know you've cleared your plate.' At the mention of Dad, I'm so relieved I decide not to challenge her, and apply myself to my miniscule meal, wondering how many minutes I can possibly make it last, even on a full stomach.

At seven o'clock, which was chimed daintily from at least five different rooms of the house, the woman who is my grandmother turns to me and says,

'Right then. Up to bed you go.' I stare at her. She is serious; I have not yet seen her smile. I say: 'I'm twenty-seven.' She nods, and tuts, and gets up from her chair and switches off the kitchen light.

'There we go,' she says. 'You're not missing out on anything down here.' In the sudden darkness she seems bigger somehow. Her voice sounds harder, and I can imagine her angry now, angry in the way that women are only angry with children when the door is closed. She says, 'I hope you're not going to cause me any trouble.'

'Where's my dad?' I say. 'Is he coming soon?' I hear how very young I sound, how small in the strange, dark house. She clicks her fingers at me, so close to my face it makes me jump, and I go meekly upstairs, back to the little nursery room where the hot water bottle is now stone cold. I don't take it out of the bed in case she sees.

I undress quickly, and when I'm done I hear her slippered footsteps on the stairs. I scramble into bed, fighting my way beneath the covers with my cold feet, and when she comes in, I am strapped in tightly up to my armpits.

'There,' she says, and goes over to the window. She turns a key in the lock on the latch and puts it in her pocket. 'All tucked up.' She draws the curtains. 'Nice and safe.' She switches out the lamp so I can barely make her out; there is only the faint orange glow coming from the hallway underneath the door. She lifts a little nursery chair and sets it at the foot of my bed. 'Safe and sound asleep in no time.'

The woman who must be my grandmother sits in the chair. She is absolutely quiet, but with every hair on my exposed arms I can feel the intensity with which she watches me, her old face unreadable, her eyes deep-set and shining. I try to lie still and breathe as naturally as possible, praying she will go, never so far from sleep in all my life. I don't know how many minutes go by like this. All the time I am listening, listening, listening for him coming, for his car in the driveway, his key in the door.

And then I hear his voice. He's laughing; his laugh is unmistakeable, even after all this time. From beneath us, I can hear the chink of glasses and plates and the faint noise of the radio. He's been here all along and I've missed him! He must be eating now, the dinner that he had meant to eat with me, drinking the wine he'd chosen specially. He must be wondering where I am and why I'm so late, looking out of the window to see me arrive at any moment, perhaps even starting to worry about me.

I don't let on that I've heard a thing. My grandmother is shifting in her chair, peering at me, and the sounds from downstairs are getting louder. There must be other people down there with my father, more people than could cram themselves into that awkward little kitchen, talking and laughing and eating. I take some silent, shallow breaths. I feel too exposed here, lying on my back. I wish I'd turned to face the wall, but it's too late for that. She gets up, and she shuffles her feet over the carpet towards me. I keep my eyes closed, but I feel the air shift as she leans over me, close, too close, only inches away.

My stomach rumbles. There's no helping it. I clench my muscles around the noise but my indignant body is unbiddable, and it seems to have no idea of the danger we're in. My eyes snap open.

'You naughty girl,' she hisses in my ear. 'But you can't fool me. I know a fake sleeper when I see one.' She turns as if to sit back down.

'Dad!' I call out, my voice so high and quiet it barely carries. 'Dad! Dad – I'm up here!'

She twists the other way. Though I can barely make out the murky shape of her, I know the movement is weird. There's something wet about it, like the way that hair moves underwater, and it's too fast. And then she is across the room and closing the door behind her and turning the key in the lock with an awful 'click'.

'No!' I force my body out of bed, my limbs numb with pins and needles, and I hammer on the door, but this too sounds muffled, and the laughter and the talk downstairs is so loud I know they'll never hear me. I shake the door handle. I kick at it. I am crying hot, powerless tears and I know she is still standing there, silently guarding me from the other side.

The phone rings. It's not my iPhone, but an old-style landline, and I grope my way towards the sound and find it, vibrating slightly on the bedside table. I lift the receiver to my ear.

'Dad?' I say? 'Dad is that you?'

'It's alright, sweetheart,' he says, and I know his voice so well that I cry harder. 'There's nothing to be afraid of.'

'She won't let me come and see you, Dad,' I sob, and I'm holding the phone so tightly it is hurting my hand.

'Don't worry, Sophie,' he says, and behind him I can still hear the other voices, and there's music, like a party now in full swing. 'I've got my eye on you. I've always kept an eye on you.'

The line crackles. His voice is distorting, and the crackle is so loud that I can't hear him anymore. The sound is coming not from the phone, but from the door. I walk towards it. There is still a glow of light beneath it, but the keyhole is completely dark. I kneel, and here the crackle is almost deafening. It's like a radio tuned between stations, or the blank sound of a walkie-talkie, or the hiss of a baby monitor. I look through it, braced for the horror of the glinting eye, and though there is something dark and gleaming, I realise it is not an eye. It is a wide-open mouth.

'Sleep tight,' comes my father's voice, barely audible through the static. 'I'll see you very soon.'

Customer Reviews for Ashley Wiccan's WonderLust Love Potion

LITTLE-GREY-WITCH

Very nice to work with. Just 2 days and my boyfriend started being sweet to me again. Thank you.

KRISTA

SUCH a pretty bottle. I love this potion so much and I KNOW it is going to start working soon ☺

TIFFANY

I ordered Ashley's love potion not for shallow reasons of lust but to reconnect with my daughter who is 15.

I want to start putting this in her food so that she'll remember who's really most important in her life and that is me and not her friends who are mostly little slags who don't even show me basic respect.

I received this package okay but the seller didnt put enough postage on my parcel and I had to pay extra before the Post Office would deliver it. Also when I opened it the bottle was cracked!!! I can't use it because the potion might have been contaminated and of course I can't risk giving that to my daughter.

I really think Ashley should ask customers what they want the potion for. It's all very well people trying to get a boyfriend and just have sex but is it too much to ask for people buying it for selfless reasons to get the best service??

I'm disappointed and would like a refund – or maybe a

replacement if Ashley can send it quickly and NOT damaged this time.

EMERALD666
BEFORE WORK MY HUBBY KEPT KISSING ME AND ASKING FOR HUGGS LOL HE IS NEVER LIKE THAT WOW!!

TIFFANY
Thank you for resending me the potion, although I must say I thought your note was a bit passive aggressive. Your tone was unnecessary and frankly not good customer service at all. Thank you for the potion but I did note that it seemed to be a different colour and consistency to the first one, it is much thicker and a very dark murky colour but the first one was much more pink. I hope that doesn't mean you've given me a dud batch, that really would be the icing on the cake with my customer experience of this seller!!!

I hope this potion works and is as powerful as people on here say my daughter has a new boyfriend and they are so rude to me it's like she's rubbing it in my face that she loves him more than me. I've tried everything, I've told her he can't come over and I confiscate her phone to make sure we get quality time together but she just wants to stay in her room.

ROSE-ROSE-RED
Ashley is very plesant to speak to and customer service is A+++. The love potion started working before it even shipped! Ps. don't know what some other people are saying

about the colour mine is a lovely pale pink

TIFFANY

Today is the first day I've been using Ashley's love potion. I put it in my daughter's cereal and even though she sometimes tries to skip breakfast or just have toast or fruit she knows shes not allowed so she ate it all and I know because I watched her. I know she can't have thrown it up again because she's not allowed to go to the toilet for 30 mins after any meal and I make sure she stays with me constantly during that time, or if she does get desperate for a wee then I have to go with her. I also put some drops in the smoothie she takes to school and 5 drops in her chicken casserole and the recommended dose is only 4 drops so it definitely should be working by now.

I watched her v closely when she got home but there was no difference so I'm very disappointed in this product so far. Her bedtime is 8pm but she went up at 7.30 because I was so upset that she didn't show me anymore affection or ask me about my day so I told her to get out of my sight. It is 10pm now and I can hear her moving about up there a bit more than usual but I don't think that's a sign of anything.

MISS-RASPBERRY

there is definitely something going on with me since using Ashley's love potion. i walked into a very smart café recently and the entire place seemed to go hushed and were paying attention to me. a group of men at a nearby table kept shooting glances at me the entire time.

no, i did not imagine it because my brother and his

girlfriend noticed it too

TIFFANY

Well I have to say that I am very surprised and pleased with what has happened and I was not expecting it after all the problems I've had with this seller.. But I've been using the love potion on my daughter for 3 days now and the difference is remarkable. For the last 6-8 months she has been very sullen and distant with me but this morning she brought me a cup of tea in bed and last night she sat right next to me on the sofa and held my hand while we were talking like she used to do when she was little and it was so sweet. When I had to leave the room she even said she missed me! so thank you, Ashley – it seems you can at least mix potions even if customer service is not your strong point! ;-)

Anyone buying this product should be aware that it is weaker than described. I've had to use 3x the recommended dose to get these results.

Also, some of you have been commenting on my reviews saying that Im too controlling and not a good mother. Well I must say that if you think a 15-year-old girl should not be close to her mother then you are not very good parents yourselves.

I think Maisie will break up with her boyfriend now if I ask her.

INCELNO.9

This post has been removed because it breached our community guidelines.

INCELNO.9
bitches

TIFFANY

I'm posting again so soon because I'm not sure Ashley's love potion has been working in the way I want after all and I don't want other buyers to be misled.

The school called me today because M was very upset. She'd been sitting in a maths lesson and started crying and asking for me and when they sent her to the nurses office to calm down she started screaming 'mummy! mummy!' and she got herself so worked up she made herself sick. It was all down the front of her uniform when I picked her up.

As soon as she saw me she was instantly a lot better and she ran up and hugged me. I thought she really does hate maths and maybe she just needed a cuddle from her mum and tbh I was a bit angry with the school for not calling me straight away. But then when I was taking her home she started some strange behaviour and I cant find any of these side effects on the label.

We got in the car and she wanted to sit next to me. I usually make her sit in the back for safety but I said ok just this once as a special treat. While I was driving she kept trying to hold my hand and when I said stop it its dangerous she started hitting herself across her chest and screaming. But not like a normal person scream, like a weird animal sort of scream, like that noise monkeys or parrots make in documentaries when a predator comes into the jungle. I had to let her hold onto my hair to get her to be quiet and when

64

she thought I wasn't looking she kept sniffing it and trying to put it in her mouth.

She's been a lot calmer since we got home and I'm crossing my fingers these side effects are only temporary because I've given her the potion in her dinner again and Im dreading taking her to school tomorrow in case she makes another scene!

TIFFANY
!!!! DO NOT IGNORE THIS REVIEW!!!!

If you are thinking of using this potion on somebody you care about then be VERY careful because you cannot predict what it's going to do to them. I've been using it on my daughter Maisie for 1 week and although it has been very effective there have also been some side effects that haven't been desirable.

Yesterday evening we were watching coronation st together and she kept asking to sit on my lap. At first I said no youre too heavy because she is 15 and quite tall and I have always been a very petite person. But she kept on asking so in the end I said ok, just for a minute. She sits on me but is obviously too heavy and I start to get pins and needles so I said Maisie get off now, you can hold my hand instead. She wouldn't move, so I tried pushing her, and then I felt my lap getting really warm and I realised she was weeing on me, just right through her clothes and all over my leggings. It was like she was marking her territory. It was horrible!

so obviously when I realised what was happening I yelled and pushed her off but she grabbed hold of my arm and took this huge bite out of the fleshy bit and there was lots of blood and I passed out for a minute so I cant be sure but I think she actually chewed it up and swallowed it

Ive locked her in her room now and ive put a bandage on my arm but there really is quite a big chunk of flesh missing and obviously i cant go to the hospital because they would want to know what happened.

I do plan to keep using the potion because my daughter's love is the most important thing to me but I do think Ashley's potions should come with a warning if this is the sort of thing that can happen. Luckily I am an experienced practitioner and I can use potions like this responsibly.

I can hear M banging on the door now. I may have to try Ashley's sleeping solution to calm her down but I know this seller's delivery is very hit and miss and also I dont think the packaging for it looks very nice.

Mr Thornton's Mother

After Elizabeth Gaskell's North and South

I

Mr Thornton's mother sleeps in the bedroom next to ours. She often sits up late, and when she does eventually climb the stairs, feeling her way in the dark to save the candle, I know by the creak and then the silence of the floorboards that she stands outside our door, listening.

When I've heard her do this, I don't like to touch that door the next morning. I imagine that she stands so close her breath fogs the surface of the wood; that I can see traces of her face powder left in the grain, stubborn specks of cotton white. I never sleep well on those nights, once I've heard her out there, breathing meanly in the dark.

II

When I first came here, still blissful from our honeymoon, my husband's mother and I kept a respectful distance from each other. This had been her home – hers and his – for so long, and I planned to assert myself gently on it, over time. Every room bore the marks of her; her austere furnishings, her old-fashioned china, her initials curled tightly around her son's in the corner of every sheet and tablecloth. After the first month, I set one of the housemaids the task of unpicking them, but there they stayed, every time my husband and I climbed into bed, like a stain; like writing on paper imprinted with someone else's handwriting.

She never calls my husband anything but John. No 'love' or 'dear', not even when she thinks they can't be overheard.

Just 'John', she says, with that look of hers, with that 'I am the mother that bore you' look. As if she'd stuff him back up in there if she could. I bet she suckled him 'til he was seven. Jesus, I bet he can *remember* it.

'John', I heard her murmur to him early one morning, as they took their usual breakfast together before the mill opened at the crack of dawn. I watched them from the still-dark corridor, and saw her clasp up her son's hand from where it lay on the table, and press it to her thin, wet mouth in adoration, and as she did it she let out a little whimper, like an animal in pain.

'No one loves me,' I am almost sure I heard him soothe her. 'No one cares for me but you, Mother.'

III

My husband doesn't seem to mind the fact his mother hates me. I think he quite enjoys himself, being caught between two women. Perhaps he hoped that married life would be peppered with our little struggles, over who gets to mend his shirts, and who tells the new cook what sort of eggs he likes for breakfast. I've learned to spot how the corners of his mouth twitch when we barb each other, before he decides it's time to call 'Ladies, ladies!'.

Then he kisses his mother on the cheek, and smiles over her head at me in that way that says he'll make it up to me later, when we are alone. What this really means is that he'll glance hopefully at me, once, before he finishes, like a schoolboy wanting praise for eating all his vegetables, and I'll give him a smile and a delicate little moan to spare his feelings. I'm sure he wonders if she's listening.

IV

My early attempts to shift Mrs Thornton, like a spider that will scuttle away to a dank corner of the attic once its cobwebs have been cleared, had no effect. If anything, her power in the house seemed to spread, and harden. I began to feel suffocated by her overwhelming presence; the ceaseless noise of the mill's machines, the fluff she brought in on her skirts that clung to everything, the chiming of the bells that summoned our servants to her, the only mistress they would ever recognise, all seemed to be extensions of her personality, malevolently reaching out their hands into every space I moved in, and taking hold.

This room, in particular, is her domain. Her smell lingers on the fabrics, all cut from her son's cloth, all spun under her unforgiving gaze. Here, she receives his guests and answers his letters, signing them 'Mrs Thornton' in that unwavering signature. In here, I will always be an intruder; a guest who has outstayed their welcome, who must accept her little kindnesses with gratitude and shame.

'Another cake, Margaret? We must satisfy your appetite, mustn't we?'

IV

Once, I walked in on my mother-in-law when she was bathing, just as she was lowering herself into the hot bath that had been meant for me. She did not blush. Her long, blueish limbs did not look capable of flushing; there was nothing soft or vulnerable about the body beneath her corsets. Her breasts hung oddly from her hard frame, like they were someone else's, like they stayed there only because

69

she commanded it.

She looked me right in the eye, and said, 'Get out. Get out, stupid girl, and close the door.'

VI

My own boy will be born in spring, when the ground will soften and I can imagine the cotton in the streets outside is cherry blossom, scenting the air rather than choking it.

She cannot have him. He is flesh of my flesh, and a mother's love holds fast, and forever. I will teach him to hate her, in ways his father will not be subtle enough to notice. Even if she lives to be a hundred, for if anyone can live on spite then she can, he is mine. He is mine, and she will never take him from me.

The Mark

I am going to climb the mountain. I've taken off my clothes, because there's no one here to see me, and I've torn them into strips. I've knotted them to make one long stretch of fabric. I've made a little bundle. I've tied it at the small of my back and wrapped it round my waist, crossing, left over right, where my hips can take the weight. The bundle against my chest, then crossed again, over my shoulders, knotted at the back of my neck. It feels secure enough. I'm afraid of being naked like this, out in the open, but I must take it with me and I will need my hands free.

I climb. I can walk upright for a few hundred feet, and then the ground veers up so steeply that I have to dip to all fours. The sandy tufts of grass give way to bare rock. Behind me, the sun, still low, spilling its warmth over the camp. I have to move quickly.

I can feel my muscles groaning as they adjust to the rhythm of this movement. I'm tired and weak. Momentum carries me up and up and I must be careful not to stop if I can avoid it. I won't be able to trust myself to start again.

Already, I can feel my knees shaking. The joints in my arms and hands feel oddly loose. With every effort, the drop beneath me stretches deeper. How would it feel, to fall now? Or now? Or at a hundred feet higher? Weightless for a glorious moment, before the impact.

I can remember vividly the only death I've ever seen. We called him Uncle. There had been an injury, decades earlier, although it didn't kill him, not for years. Rumour has it he was fearsome in those battles; too strong and too fast for their rusting weapons, too clever to be outsmarted by their little beeping boxes. That's how they tell it, the older ones, in their stories. Soft, slow, furless men who carried flashing tools that bleep!bleep!ed when they saw us coming, like frightened birds.

Not battles, Dad said. Skirmishes. There weren't enough of them left for anything you could call a battle. But they were vicious in the stories Isi used to tell me. He was old enough to know better, Dad said once, after he'd been woken up again by my grasping little arms, winding themselves around his neck. Whimpering about a nightmare.

But Isi had never been too old for anything. He'd been telling me about the Crab Men, who had shells on their backs that grew from their spines, which you had to break with a hammer if you wanted to kill them. They could only move sideways. The Crab Men were among my least favourite of Isi's stories. Only the Silencers were worse.

Uncle's death had made no sense. I remember laughing at Dad's grey face. I remember dangling from his arm, reaching up and tugging his beard, trying to make him smile. I remember that I stopped laughing, when I saw his expression reflected all around me.

They didn't know what to do. They'd never buried anyone. They lay Uncle down on a stretcher supported by two rocks. It was so strange, seeing him turned cold and limp, like an animal. I thought he looked like something we'd hunted. I wondered if we had to eat him.

The effort of this climb is reassuring. It's a surprise to me that my limbs will move at all, when, in the night, I'd been so sure I'd finish up cold and limp like Uncle. I'd thought about going back to our hut. Waking Hetan, saying, Please, don't make me do this on my own. But I needed to be far from the camp. And in the end, I hated the thought of it, him watching this monster swell and then split open, spilling its juices on the ground.

The splitting open didn't kill me. I'm here and I'm conscious and I can hear the sucking and blowing of my lungs. In and out. Higher and higher. The fine, dark hair on my body is dank with sweat, but the wind up here is drying me. My arms and shoulders are remembering their strength, though I can't stop trembling. I have to remind myself: It doesn't matter. No more than my nakedness matters, up here, alone. The hard skin on my feet is aware of the unfamiliar ground it navigates, but though it smarts a little, it's too strong and thick to break. Up and up and up, toes stretching to find purchase in smaller and less certain footholds. There's nobody to watch the method of my ascent.

The rock is dry. A ledge gives way beneath my hand, just as I'm shifting my weight. A heart-lurching sway out into nothingness before lunging back, scrabbling painfully for a new grip. The flesh on my hand opens. I stare at it. I think the word, *wound*. I feel like my body is escaping itself.

I press my forehead against the mountain and give a low growl of relief. Distance is all that matters now. I've got to keep moving. Get beyond the territory, where they'll never follow. There's still blood, dripping down my legs. It isn't finished with me yet.

The mark was something I stayed in happy ignorance of

73

for the first years of my life. I was like any child. I took my body for granted and assumed it was like all the others. We had an understanding, Dad and I, that I wouldn't take my clothes off to go swimming. I don't know what excuse I made, or if I even had to make one, any of those times the youngest of us (and there weren't many, then, we not-quite-men) would leap, whooping, from the over-hanging branches into the river. Perhaps with Isi beside me, no one dared poke fun. More than twice my age and, at that time, nearly three times my size, he could have flattened anybody who made an issue of the way Dad kept me swaddled up. But for those long, earliest years, I thought nothing of it. We were too busy being the boys let loose about the camp, all brothers together.

A bit deformed, they used to say. Something not quite right, but they couldn't put their finger on it. Something gone a bit wrong, in that container where they made me. If only they knew how wrong I'd gone.

The bundle has started screaming, and it won't stop.

Uncle must have known, I think. I asked him once, not long before he stopped speaking, who would make the new ones if he couldn't. He shook his head. There were enough of us, he told me, already too many mouths to feed, no more fighting or disease to thin us out. But I always suspected that he might have gone on, if it hadn't been for the mistake – whatever it was – he made with me. I've lived with the shadow of that thought for a long time. There'll be no more of us, and it's because of me.

That mark between my legs, that strange, creviced fingerprint. If they find me, they'll know it all. They mustn't

74

find me.

The mountain hates me. The hot wind buffets me against its unyielding surface and leaves my ears ringing. We are born to climb, it's the most natural of things; but this enormous mound of earth doesn't welcome me like a tree would. It wants rid of me; this small black flea, crawling on its back.

I drink from a tiny stream of water that trickles out of the mountain before disappearing into the rock. I slurp there for what feels like a very long time. But my thirst still nags at me, scratching my throat. Soon, I know, it will become overwhelming.

I wet my fingers and poke them into the bundle's mouth. It wails, unsatisfied, uncomprehending. I'm sorry, little one. I don't know what to do.

I have to keep climbing.

Dad had to tell me, eventually. He made me sit on the floor and held a mirror up in front of me. He told me to look between my legs. I saw the mark, and I noticed for the first time that it wasn't what I was supposed to have. Other children, other people, were all made one way, and I had to make do with this ugly imprint of wrongdoing. It'll be better if we keep it secret. If the others see it, they might be frightened. I don't know what they'd do. How long he'd been carrying that burden, all on his own. He looked almost relieved to pass it on to me.

Then the blood started. It was muddy, at first. I thought I might have soiled myself, although it smelled different. For a few months, it came and went. I washed twice, three times a day sometimes, sitting nervously at mealtimes, waiting for an opportunity to subtly swipe a hand between my legs and check the colour of my fingers. But then it came for real. A great griping pain in my belly had me crouching in the river, chattering and moaning like I'd eaten something bad. Others had passed by and laughed at me, crying and shitting so openly. I swore at them, tucking my lip over my gums and baring my teeth. Shit off. I needed the water to hold me or my guts would fall out.

When I finally stood up, the water running down my thighs was a bright, dangerous crimson.

Dad didn't know what to do. Isi turned pale when I showed him the bandages I'd had to wrap myself in. It stopped, after a few miserable days, but it came back again. There was no Uncle to ask, no other medic we dared tell it to. I shuddered when I thought what they might do to me, in one of those huts where machines still flickered and buzzed, where the few species of animal we didn't eat were occasionally taken and dissected. What would that curiosity do to me?

So it had to be dealt with. An unpleasant symptom of that strange way I'd been formed, another facet of the half-secret that I was not quite normal. It didn't seem that likely it would kill me, coming and going as it did. It just had to be endured. And once a month I would lock myself in our hut and curl up in my bunk and think sore, furious thoughts as I listened to the games being won and lost outside, without me.

The sun is making its presence felt now. I can feel the individual hairs on the back of my neck as if they're needles. My breathing hurts. Something from the bundle has come loose and dangles down, sticking wetly to my thigh. It doesn't look like part of the creature, but it's stuck to him, right in the centre. Horrible, slimy thing. Had it always been inside me? Did I need it – is that why I won't stop bleeding?

If I look behind me, I can see the dirty, spotted trail I've left behind, staining its path all the way down. How many feet of blood now? I should have been trying to cover my tracks. What if they see it, and follow?

We had a cat once. A mystery to everyone where it might have come from, but too old and small and sickly to be worth eating. Its fur was thin and matted. It had clusters of tumours in its ears.

The medics took no interest. The oldest in the camp had seen cats before, occasionally, when there used to be more of them. No one knew how this one had survived so long, and some of the other men were afraid of it. Isi tried to tell me that the Crab Men's favourite food was cats, and they'd come looking for it, but he was only jealous because the cat and I were friends at once.

I'd spotted him in a tree and swung myself up to join him, and so it began – and continued – on Cat's terms. He opted to sleep on my bunk most nights. I opted to let him.

One day, there was no sign of him anywhere. He'd disappeared before, but this time I had a dark feeling, and I went about the camp calling for him as dusk fell. That night, I crawled to Isi's bunk, to feel the comfort of another breathing thing, but he wouldn't stop his scary stories, and I dreamt of the Silencers. According to my brother, they were a race of men who looked like us except for their long, hard tails, and their forked tongues. They didn't speak. They only hissed, and that is how you heard them coming.

He said: when Uncle was a child, he'd lain awake at night, listening for the sound of a Silencers raid. That hiss would fall over the camp; a noise you might try to mistake for crickets at first, but which would soon grow into the furious shaking of a hundred rattlesnakes. If you lived, it was a sound you'd never be able to forget.

Nonsense, Uncle used to say. They were only men. But a shadow would pass over him.

We couldn't find Cat for several days, and I was certain that the Silencers had taken him. But finally he was discovered, still and peaceful, hidden in the grating underneath the generator.

It happens, Dad said. Some creatures know when their time is up, and they just want to be alone. They weren't like us, whose time is never up, whose days are numberless.

The little bundle wails and sleeps, wails and sleeps. His heart is fluttering wildly; I can feel it, with him strapped against my ribcage. He's the only baby (for I suppose that's what he must be) I've ever seen since I was one, so I don't know if this is normal. Perhaps I should have left him behind. Perhaps I should leave him now, here, in his wrappings. The sound of his cry is urgent and accusing. Too bad, for him, that we've been landed with each other. Too bad he had a monster for an incubator.

I've reached an impasse. The climb is so steep now it actually tilts back on itself. The overhang feels like the mountain leering at me. Above me, straight ahead and to either side, the hand and footholds thin out and disappear. There is a small ridge, up and to my left, perhaps six feet away. Three months ago I could have jumped it, if my nerve held out. But now I've got no faith in this shaking, sweating body. I'll stumble. I'll fail. I'm getting weaker with every minute that the sun beats down. I can feel the grip of my hands already loosening, desperate for relief. My toes break their cramped hold and I fall into a dead hang. If I stay here much longer, the result will be the same.

I set my sights on that ridge. I think I'd rather die leaping for it than hang here, feeling my limbs weaken, waiting to plummet. The rock between us is interspersed with tiny cracks. None big enough to support more than a finger or a toe, but just maybe, at speed…

I can't think any longer, or I won't do it. I use the remaining strength in my thigh muscles to propel me upwards, scrabbling at the surface of the cliff with my hands and feet, crawling almost vertically, feeling stones dislodge and crumble as I scrape my way along. Faster, faster, and I almost have it, my left leg straining up at an impossible angle, gripping with my toes, feeling something twist and snap. Hauling myself up, almost crushing the bundle in the process. It whimpers, or that might be me, my own mouth gaping open.

I think I'm still alive. My leg feels numb and limp, but I think I must be.

I'm glad Hetan can't see me now. A funny thought; I'm not sentimental, not really. But my thirst is turning into dizziness and my mind is drifting. I liked the smell of him. I liked the scratch of his beard on my shoulder when he wrapped his arms around me.

I can't explain it. I can't say clearly what it was or how our

79

bodies knew it. I only know that I was dark and joyful and animal, and I felt absolutely no shame. My thoughts weren't words again until much, much later, and then they only said to me: This must be how some men are meant to love each other.

Animal. That's right, I think. They're so few and far between now, their names have mostly been forgotten. But I've seen, once or twice, a rare kill examined by the camp, a strange sort of hush descending. What is it? Its hind legs pulled apart.

My father had companions, sometimes. It was in the usual way of things, though some men never did it. Some would creep in and lie beside him for a night or two, and Isi and I would hear them murmuring after all was quiet. Others would stay longer. Some of them would come to our hut and stay for years.

It was Josef, when I was very small. I would fall asleep against the fur of his chest, and he would pick the lice from my back, just like Dad did. One of my earliest memories is of watching Josef eat. I was sitting on his stomach in the sunshine, watching him peel fruit with his long, clever toes, staring as he passed it from foot to hand to mouth. Trying to intercept it, snatching the pieces as they passed me. Him, playing at defeat with every other mouthful. The warm, sweet fruit, spiked with the salt from his skin.

He sleeps beside someone else now. I've sometimes wondered if it was my secret that sent him away: the telling or the not telling of it.

Something has fallen out of me. That queasy, rolling ache began again and I came juddering to a halt on this ledge, pressing myself flat and feverish against the mountain as the rush of it overtook the horrible twitching of my injured leg.

Please, not again. Please not again. I'll die, I'll die.

It isn't a creature though, this time. It is a piece of meat. I am relieved at first, if you can call it that. When the new spasms start, I wonder how many little beasts there are inside me. I imagine there are hundreds, squirming and jostling in my stomach, clawing to get out. I imagine the agony of it, repeated over and over, as they each break free. I am so happy, when it comes, that this one makes no sound.

But then it occurs to me, in the heady aftermath of fresh pain, that it might have tried to be another creature after all. A poor, malformed thing, gone even more wrong than I did. I turn the red-brown mass over and over in my hands, looking for anything that might have been a hand, a shoulder, a mouth.

The bundle is screaming again, writhing weakly in its fabric sling. I'm still holding the bloody lump, but I'm sure it's formless. It looks like an organ from the inside of an animal; a liver, or a heart. It looks like food. I must be hungry, but the feeling is distant, somewhere far off in my bleeding, pumping body where I can't reach it.

I let the lump slip, greasy, from my hands and fall away. Somewhere down the cliff beneath me, I suppose it will catch and clot. Some animal scavenger will find it. We've always known they're out there still, these invisible refugees, roaming on two or four legs and making off with things in the dead of night. I feel light and hollow now, though my belly still sticks strangely out in front of me, grazing the cliff-face. I think I must be empty.

Now that I've stopped, I can hear mad noises in the gaps between the gusts of wind. I close my eyes, and Isi comes and mutters in my ear, and I tell him, Not that story! but he goes on anyway. I'm being watched. Something is following me, and it knows the mountain better than I do. Men from the camp have found me gone and are hunting me, poised to destroy this demon that lived secretly among them.

I need to rest. Just a few moments. Just to let me catch my breath. A brown line has appeared on my skin, clearly visible beneath the fine hair. Like someone's smudged it there with dirty fingers, from the mark right up the centre to my chest, which is stiff and swollen. However hard I rub, it won't come off. Oh help me, what is happening to me?

I can hardly see the camp anymore. That's good: even if they look up here I'd barely be a speck to them. No one will see my little shadow on the rock and think, Our man is there. It's the furthest I've ever been from home.

The weight of the bundle is small but constant. All there. I checked. No mark on him, just everything normal, everything in miniature. A tiny little man, whose skull I could cup in the palm of my hand.

From this height, the land around me is transformed. The woods that separate the camp from the rest of the valley are much narrower than I ever thought, barely a divide at all. I can see the point at which the river bends, reveals itself, and joins the sea. Everything small, and arbitrary, from this vantage point. So meaningless. So accidental.

They'll ask Hetan, I suppose, when they can't find me. Then they'll ask Dad and Isi. All of them will suspect, but none of them will know, that something bad has happened to me. Those last few months of my body stretching out of all proportion, barely concealable under my clothes. Those strange, worried looks as I lumbered about the camp, feeling sick if I strained myself, getting too heavy to run. I'd always been rounded, though whether that was due to my natural shape or part of my deformity, we'd never been sure.

Hetan. What will he do? If he tells them just how sick I was, they'll ask him how, they'll ask him why they didn't know, why I didn't ask for help. If I were my father, would I have done what he did? Is it the mark of a man to speak the truth, or to keep his secrets safe?

I'm moving again, though so slowly that my progress is barely worth the effort. My left leg is useless. The sky is getting dark now, though it can't be midday yet.

I can almost see the summit. The air up here is cold and fresh as it enters my parched mouth. All around me is the sky. I've never seen so much of it. Cloudless, aching, opaque blue. I feel like it couldn't harm me. I could let go now, relax the grip of my burning, blistering digits and sink down into it. I would float out from the mountain like the sky was cool water. It would wash the dusty blood from my skin and hair.

The bundle is quiet at last; it knows we're safe here. But I want to reach the top. It's a compulsion, now we've come this far. I want to look down the mountain from its highest point, just once, before I give in.

But there's a sound. It's been rising for a while now, just beneath the roar of the altitude in my ears and my own rough breathing, tugging at the edges of my attention. A low hiss, growing louder, growing nearer. Like crickets, like a hundred angry rattlesnakes. Coming this way.

There's nowhere to hide myself. The sweat in my eyes has blurred my vision, and the glare of the sun is painful, reflected on the rock and my own raw hands in front of me. It must be an hour since I've looked directly up, and as I do it now the tendons in my neck shriek at the unfamiliar effort. The bundle feels like a dead weight, anchoring me to the mountain. I can't move quickly; even the fear can't inspire anything but this agonising, creeping pace. That hideous hiss, getting louder, seeking me out…

Where can I hide? I imagine I can hear footsteps beneath the hissing, perhaps even the swish of a tail. It's coming from all around me, it seems nearer whichever way I crawl. I squint, and imagine I can see a pale face emerging from a precipice above me, a forked tongue flicking from between thin lips. It shouldn't matter, I suppose, if this is how it ends. But I picture them dragging my sore and swollen body back down the mountain after all this effort. The pain of what they might do to me: this monstrous exile of a race that used to slaughter them. Dismemberment, or worse, if I'm still alive to feel it.

For the first time now, the tears are starting to flow. Toxic, self-pitying tears, burning the skin they touch. I only wanted to end in a peaceful place. I wanted, so badly, to lay myself flat beneath the sky, and let go of my dry, finished body.

A bird circles overhead. A vast, brown shape I've never seen before, swooping with what looks like joy. The bird must see, from up there, what lies beyond the mountain. Perhaps there are more of its kind there. Perhaps the wasteland is smaller, like the forest, than we thought. Perhaps, if we could see far enough, we'd find more of us.

I'm cold. We've made it so far, the bundle and I. This journey together, this pilgrimage to take us out of the world. The hissing doesn't feel so loud now. I can't be afraid, I haven't got the energy. I long to sleep.

My body sags heavier into the dust. Gravity pulls at my tired back, it says, Soon. Soon. My weak leg doesn't pain me at all.

A hand on my arm, and then another. Hoisting me, because the mountain beneath me falls away. A voice, rattling gently, though I can't hear the words.

I think I'm being touched all over. I think the touch is gentle.

Rosie

I wasn't supposed to be left unsupervised with Rosie. But her handlers had clocked off for the evening and the rest of the crew were tucked up in their trailers, so I seized my chance for some alone time.

At first, I only watched her. She'd been my body double and my muse for nearly eight months, but still I found her inexhaustibly fascinating. I sat opposite her—a weaker, paler mirror image—and watched as she toyed with a piece of melon rind, her fingernails picking at tiny pieces of its remaining flesh and bringing them to her lips. The movement of her hands was like the movement of an exquisite automaton: so unlikely. So startlingly true to life.

Monkey school, we called it; all our doubles were really apes. We treated them like celebrities. We spent our time off-camera photographing them and begging to be allowed to hug them, just this once. But none of them were quite as clever as my Rosie, who knew me and rushed to meet me in the mornings, who always got the best takes, who was first back into her crate when it was time to wrap for the day. I was smitten. I could be forgiven, surely, for this illegal visit, given just how much I loved her.

Every few seconds, Rosie's black eyes flicked up as she checked on me. After fifteen minutes, she huffed out a breath of acknowledgement and shuffled closer.

I mimicked her. It was habit now; she moved, I moved. We rolled our shoulders up and back. Our knuckles kneaded the concrete floor to pitch our weight forwards. I'd wondered if she'd recognise me without my prosthetics, but the connection between us made my scalp fizz. Her expression was like a book written in a foreign language; I knew there was great meaning hidden there if I only I could read it.

Earlier that day, we'd had to stop shooting for an hour because something had upset the apes. We'd watched Rosie with another chimp, a more nervous creature than my counterpart, as they shot a scene in which they had to jump down, threatening and ready for battle, from the roof of a stationary train carriage. The other actors and I were waiting to take our turn, sweating inside our furry costumes. We were just changing places when one of the camera guys leapt out at me wearing a gorilla mask, howling in my face and pounding his fists against his chest. I jumped and made him bellow with laughter, then he slapped me on the back and wandered off to find someone else to shock.

It had only been a joke, but Rosie didn't know that. A split second after her handler had clanked shut the door of her travel cage, Rosie screamed and threw her whole weight in the direction of the masked cameraman. Her handler yelled and toppled backwards. Rosie was inconsolable with rage; she wrenched at the bars, yanking backwards and forwards so she almost tipped the crate on its side, and her screeching set off all the other apes. From what seemed like every corner of the set they screamed and hammered and bashed themselves against the bars and walls of their little prisons like they'd all gone instantly mad, and their handlers stared at each other in shock before they set off between the animals with their electric prods, jabbing mercilessly until the rebellion subsided.

What happened? they asked. *What set them off?* Nobody seemed to know. I kept my mouth shut, but as they wheeled Rosie away I watched her slumped, dark body get smaller and smaller with a potent mixture of love and shame. She had been trying to defend me; I was certain of it. She had been hurt because of me, and somehow, I had to make it right between us.

Crouched on the floor of the trailer, I let Rosie's solemn gaze engulf me. We were almost nose to nose. She pressed her beautiful, so-nearly-human face against the bars so that her soft lips bulged between them. I pushed my own forwards, imagining her strength in my jaw. Beneath us both, her breasts hung smooth and slack, long dark nipples dipping into the fur of her belly. We breathed together: in, and out. I could see my own rapture reflected in her pupils.

Forgetting all my training, I reached out to touch her. She took my hand in hers and I felt the warm leather of her palm, the maternal pressing of her fingertips. It felt like a blessing. Rosie's face might have been the face of God.

But then she pulled. Her grip on my hand tightened, and she dragged my arm towards her chest, forcing my whole body up against the bars with ease. She didn't break eye contact, but her mouth opened to emit a short shriek—in pleasure or anger, I couldn't tell. I tried to tug my arm back from her, but the attempt was useless.

With her magnificent strength she carried my fingers up towards her mouth, and into it.

I didn't dare move. Not with the pressure of her teeth beneath my thumb and her powerful grip around my wrist. Her eyes looked out at me, so shockingly familiar that I could almost believe she was another actor in a costume if it weren't for those great grunting breaths. I prepared myself for pain, for the snapping of my bones, for the hot gush of blood when she bit down into my fingers. I could survive without a hand, it occurred to me. And in the awful, inevitable horror of this thought, I broke our connection at last, and closed my eyes.

In the darkness of my own skull, I felt a shift. My panic drained down and out of me, and in its place I felt the growth of something powerful and wordless. My shoulders sank in their sockets and thickened. My pelvis widened, and my breath deepened into the promise of strength, hot and sour in my nostrils, as through drawn from a furnace. In my huge mouth I could feel the fragile bones of my own puny fingers. I saw myself: not a mirror image but a pale, mocking shadow. A half thing. A thing that would not need a cage or a cattle prod to be kept quiet and safe.

In my own body, somewhere very far away, I felt Rosie's tongue explore my fingers, tasting each in turn. The smell of my fear was as strong as the dusty scent of her, female and earthy and both of us animals as we squatted there. There was no window through which I might be heard if I called out. No sky, no air, no light. No other creature that might distract her and save me. Until, at the same moment, we both heard the footsteps on the gravel path outside the hut, the shout of the handler who had forgotten to lock the door and returned to secure it.

I opened my eyes in time to see Rosie let my hand fall, slack, to the ground. Her steady gaze was on me still, and she watched as I crawled away, my limbs vibrating with panic. She sat like that, unmoving, quietly observing me until the door banged open. And then she fled, chattering, to the back of her cage, and turned her face to the wall, and would not look at me again. She was oblivious, of course she was, to my desperate need for a better farewell. She was just an ape.

I staggered to my feet. I took the tellings-off without a word in my defence. I'm not sure I could have spoken, and the words as I'm saying them now sound strange to me, feel strange on a tongue that tastes of sour breath and the salt of my own skin.

Lady Macbeth

Night's candles have burnt out.

The last time he touched her was the night they cleaned the gory secret from each other's skin. He trembled and shook, and she washed him like a child awakened from a nightmare.

When a man's grief takes hold, it relieves him of responsibility. A woman's is practical: there is work to be done. Hell is murky, and there were candles to be lit.

She said: 'For you I would murder the world.'

As she dressed him, guilt solidified. In him it became a passionate hobby; in her, only a tender sort of madness, like a bruise on the soul.

'A little water clears us of this deed.'

But who would have thought the old man to have had so much blood in him?

In the morning, it began: the torturous chess game to check whose heart was blackest. At breakfast she fed him blackberries – hand-picked – and mopped where the juice ran down his chin. He pushed her hand away. She raised another handful, dark and poisonous, but he would not eat. She knew the reason for his cruelty: if she was monstrous, he was not.

Wash your hands, put on your nightgown. Look not so pale…

Her as mother, or nurse – him, the ghost in their marriage – their bed dark and snug like a coffin. But still the deed felt special – this thing that they had done together. The Thane of Fife had a wife, and all his pretty ones lie in cold beds now. Ignore them suckling at her in her sleep. Ignore their grasping little fingers.

He sleeps no more. He doesn't say his prayers.

And here's the smell of blood still!

But his nightmares visit him – asleep or not. Little dead children hold his daggers to their throats; prostitutes become his witches, whispering.

'O, full of scorpions is my mind, dear wife.' She says: 'You used to look at me.'

She stops her monthly bleeding. As if her body knows she's taken children. Her hands will not come clean.

She starts to dress herself in pale silks, screaming her innocence at him in a swish of fabric. A soft sky blue glows against her skin; cream sets off the colour of her hair.

Yet here's a spot...

She may as well have dressed herself in shadow. She gets good at telling herself how fine and justifiable his abandonment of her is.

In the end, she does it neatly – outside, where the mess won't fall to other women. In her swoop, she wonders if he hears the screech of the owl, if he'll be wakeful still, pacing their floors, speaking out loud to spectres.

Too late for that now.

To bed, to bed: there's knocking at the gate.

The Gastrosophist

It took twelve waiters to carry in the centrepiece. A young Indian elephant on a great gold platter, posed as if sleeping, its trunk coiled around the carving knife on which the candlelight glinted. Silence fell as they heaved it onto the table, their expressions grim but satisfied. The camera crew crept in as closely as they dared. The guests put down their knives and waited.

The Gastrosophist, sitting at the head of the table, dabbed at his mouth with his napkin and laid it down again. The waiters melted back against the walls, sweat shining on their forearms. The chef herself, broad and sturdy-backed in her clean apron, eyed the guests. But no applause came. The mood was solemn, expectant.

'This looks very fine,' said the Gastrosophist. And he rose from his seat.

He plucked the carving knife from the coil of the elephant's trunk. The young woman beside him gave a nervous giggle, and his pale eyes swung towards her. The eyes of the cameras followed.

'Like King Arthur,' she said. 'The sword in the stone!'

He smiled at her, and she pressed her lips together, as if to keep more words from spilling out. He reached out with the blade and tested it on the beast's trunk, so that the first two inches of snout fell away in a perfect slice, the steam still rising from it.

And now the guests did applaud. An intense burst of clapping punctuated by whoops of delight. But when the carving knife rose again they all fell silent.

The Gastrosophist climbed up to stand on his gilded chair and sank the blade into the elephant's back. The hot skin crackled as it split, but did not resist him. The knife cut deep and long and came out clean. He laid it to one side and began to part the roasted flesh with his hands, one knee up against the creature's skull for leverage.

Slowly, and with much effort, the beast's back parted, and now the chef and her three helpers came forward. With much heaving and tugging there emerged, like a perverse caesarean birth, the next delicacy, framed perfectly on Camera Two: a lioness, skinned but fully clawed and toothed, her mouth propped open in a snarl.

A howl of pleasure erupted around the table. Several guests stood up to see more clearly, slapping their hands together and sharing looks of glee and awe. Their host's companion – the young woman who had spoken and who looked so lovely in her pale green gown – reached out a finger to touch the lioness's paw, and a man beside her roared in her ear as she did so, making her squeal and leap back. The air in the room thickened with the smell of meat.

The second challenge now in front of him, the Gastrosophist picked up the carving knife again. More waiters, quick and graceful with the cameras on them, stepped forward to clear space in front of him on the table. Plates of cheese and shellfish and domes of perfumed rice were carried away by deft and silent hands. Their master leaned over the flayed cat, and pressed the tip of the knife lovingly into the base of her neck. He scored downwards, the warm skin and muscle springing open easily this time, and there was murmuring and the shifting of chairs and feet as his guests craned their necks to be the first to see.

Inside the lioness, its limbs curled tightly as it lay in foetal position on its side, was a chimpanzee. Its pose was so lifelike that it almost seemed it could be sleeping, or else curling up in fear, its arms and legs tightly folded and its face tucked in.

The Gastrosophist climbed right up onto the table and he knelt astride the ape, his expression now unreadable. He looked at it for two long minutes, the carving knife balanced in his hand; a sort of bliss, perhaps, in his communion with this animal cousin as the party held its breath and waited.

He lowered the carving knife so it pointed down towards the chimp's protected belly.

'What is it?' hissed the woman in the green dress to the man who had roared at her, and he bent to whisper something in her ear that made her clutch his arm and gasp at him, her cheeks reddening. But then the chef, whose eyes were fixed as keenly on her judge as his were on the chimpanzee, gave a soft, deliberate cough.

Breaking his reverie, the Gastrosophist turned to look at her, his blade still grazing its chosen entry point. She gave the smallest shake of her head, and he turned from her to the ape again and he seemed to understand. He put aside the knife.

The Gastrosophist reached down and took the chimp's arms in his hands. He prized them apart, and there, clutched against its bosom, he found the masterpiece that made his guests cheer and stamp their feet so that their glasses clinked together and the cutlery rattled on the table.

A stillborn human baby lay there, pale and tiny, its eyes

closed and its lips ever so slightly parted. It was moist and greasy from its incubation inside the layers of roasted meat, but the fine fair hair on its head and its impossibly miniature finger and toenails gave it all the realism that was required of it. And better, more miraculously still, beneath the translucent skin of its chest could be seen a heart, artificially beating.

The Gastrosophist bent closer, the knees of his suit trousers picking up soup stains from the table. He lowered his face over the infant, so its false heartbeat almost touched his lips. The chef stepped nearer, her eyes burning, her hands wringing the sweat from each other. All around the table, the guests might have been turned to stone.

'Almost,' he said. 'It is almost perfect.'

Silt

It must have been the sea that made him.

She found him in a rock pool after the storm. He lay like harmless sludge at the bottom of her net, and she might have cast him off, had it not been for the sparkling shard of oil-green glass that had lodged itself in his belly, catching the light.

She shook his little body into the palm of her hand. Turning him gently with her finger, she picked out first the wiggling fruits of the ocean that squirmed inside him, and then the shard itself. He sighed with relief, and a tiny bubble of air rose from his small silt mouth. She was so amazed, she laughed. It was the first human sound he ever heard.

She took him home with her, and he grew. For a month she hand-reared him, this little silt creature that was neither fish nor fowl. He needed a womb, but she was afraid of him disintegrating in too much water. So, she kept him in just a few clear inches, moving him from windowsill to windowsill to give him the best of the sun. She fed him fresh sand that she sifted for shells, in pinches, then handfuls. When he got too big for the washing up bowl, he opened his eyes.

His senses sharpened. He recognised the difference between her voice and those of visitors, and for a while he would curl himself up and tremble when there was a stranger in the house. She kept him out of sight, and after a few weeks he seemed to grow in confidence; she would hear him splashing from the other room, as if attempting to join in the conversation. Once he'd graduated to the bath, it became much harder to keep him secret. A friend, stopping by for tea one afternoon, asked to use the bathroom, and was given a stilted tale of faulty plumbing, only interrupted by the unmistakeable sound of somebody pulling the plug out of a full bath. Visitors were not admitted after that.

She found him standing over the toilet, experimenting with the flush. He was an inch or so taller than her at full height, and proportionally – definitely – male. The fine grit of his skin sparkled where it was still wet, and he left faint traces of himself on everything he touched. Looking around, she saw evidence of his investigations: the sink, the toothpaste, her box of sanitary towels. The final drops of bathwater gurgled in the plughole and were gone.

He turned his mother-of-pearl eyes towards her, and she reached out to touch the firm, damp flats of his chest. He felt like fluid sandstone; like rock with a current beneath it. When she took her hand away, a thin layer of him came with it.

She said: 'What will we do?'

He pulled her head towards the place her hand had been, inviting her to listen. Inside him, she heard the drag and push of the tide.

Her Outer Self

Donna was still stewing on the horrible day she'd had when she noticed the woman on the bench. The woman was sitting off to one side of the crowded platform, beyond the reach of the cover that was protecting most of the commuters from the Manchester drizzle. She didn't look like she was interested in boarding the tram at all and didn't even look up as it slowed and stopped, and Donna watched from her privileged position in the very best seat. The one right at the end before the empty driver's compartment; the one on its own, so she didn't have to squish up next to anybody else. The one without the 'Please give up this seat' sign.

Donna was intrigued. The woman on the bench was crying, and didn't seem to notice the rain, even though it was settling on her wool coat and must have been soaking through the canvas tote bag on her lap, its damp fingers seeping in to touch whatever it was she carried. It was Donna's right to look, she reasoned. The woman should have her cry at home, if she didn't want Donna looking. The woman's head was bowed and she was resting her face in her hands as her sobs shook her; a figure of such abject angst that Donna found herself staring and staring. Who was this woman, in her pencil skirt and cheap trainers, to be so extravagantly miserable in public? There was a phone resting on top of the canvas tote, and the woman lifted one hand to jab at the wet screen with one finger, anguish evident in every poke. Only one of her eyes was visible under her fringe, and it was dark and ridiculous with smudged mascara. Donna felt a lovely sort of thrill, watching her through the tram window. It was like she was not a real person at all but a film, or an art installation, put there for Donna's amusement and to distract her from the unpleasant events of the day which she had feared, until this woman and her theatrics, was going to spoil her whole weekend.

The woman was quite young, Donna realised. She might have been her colleague Charlotte or her daughter Florrie's age – probably under thirty, anyway. She dressed older, the way people did if they could only buy clothes from charity shops, but Donna could tell her youth by the way she held herself, tense like a cowering puppy. Her long, thin hair was dyed darker than its natural colour, and there was an inch of mousey-grey visible at the roots. *Jab-jab-jab* went her fingers, her knee shaking violently up and down. Boyfriend trouble, Donna supposed. Everyone on the platform was purposefully not looking at her. Whoever he was, he was probably better off out of it.

The tram doors opened and the mass of waiting people began to shove their way into Donna's carriage. This was the awkward part about the good seat: the envious glares she got as the standing passengers arranged themselves around her. But all Donna's attention was on the crying woman. As the platform emptied and the air in the tram thickened and fogged, the woman on the bench uncurled herself from her hunched position, tilted her head back towards the half-dark sky, and *howled* in pain, her mouth wide open, her spine arched like an actress pretending to give birth.

Donna watched in fascinated horror. Then the tram doors closed, and in those seconds before it pulled away from the platform, the woman's head snapped back and she looked right back at Donna. Their eyes met with such visceral force that Donna jerked back from the window and knocked into an older woman standing just behind her, who tutted and made a show of massaging her elbow where she'd bumped it.

'Sorry!', Donna said. 'Sorry sorry.' The tutting woman pursed her lips.

Had she imagined it? The intensity of that stare, and the fury in it; as though she'd been caught prying on something lewd and private, when the stupid girl had been making a spectacle of herself in full view of at least fifty people.

Donna's tired brain was playing tricks on her because of all this rubbish with Charlotte – that was what it was. Was Charlotte, too, crying theatrically on her way home somewhere? Donna wouldn't put it past her. Charlotte was the cause of all her bad mood, after she'd made their meeting today so needlessly awkward, so long and painful, so embarrassing for all concerned.

The tram rattled along. The man standing closest to Donna staggered as the driver braked sharply, his crotch jolting uncomfortably close to Donna's face. She pulled her phone out of her pocket for something else to look at and swiped mindlessly for a moment, still picturing Charlotte's blotchy, trembling face. She wanted to call Florrie and have a good moan; her daughter owed her that at least. But it was six o'clock, and she'd be feeding or bathing the boys already, and wouldn't listen properly anyway.

The next stop was Trafford Bar, and the waiting commuters were five or six deep. The window beside Donna was beginning to mist over, and she wiped a viewhole with her sleeve, getting her usual twinge of pleasure at the sight of all those people who hadn't a hope in hell of boarding. She allowed herself a disapproving glare at the determined few who were attempting to crush themselves in through the doors, forcing the already cramped occupants into every inch of available space.

It was really starting to rain hard now. The new passengers were glistening with rain, and carrying umbrellas that dribbled onto the shoes and bags of those nearest to them, who shifted as far as they were able but pretended not to see. Most of the men and women on the platform looked resigned, and they stared down at their phones or up at the sign telling them how many minutes to the next sardine tin that might offer them a way home. But one of them, she realised, was looking straight at her, from the second row of people.

It was her. The weeping woman from the bench. The one who had given her that hard, dark look.

Donna's stomach rolled like a seal in water. She glanced up at the man above the crotch beside her. His face was shiny with grease, and he was chewing the spikes of his beard. She turned back to the window – obviously she must have been mistaken. It had fogged up again, so she rubbed it quickly with the heel of her hand. But there were still two eyes on her, still fixed and frozen. Still focusing with alarming intensity at the tram, at exactly the place where Donna was sitting.

It was definitely the same woman. Unless Donna's brain had glitched somehow, like a sort of deja vu. But no, because there was that sad little tote bag and its dampening contents; there were the smears of mascara mixing with her foundation. Her ugly coat and shoes were both a deeper colour now, and she must be getting soaked to the skin.

But she couldn't have walked here from the last tram stop so quickly, could she? Donna supposed they weren't that far away from each other, not really. Donna's pulse began to thump absurdly. The woman moved towards the tram doors, tears still marking out oily tracks down her face, never taking her eyes off Donna's window.

The standing passengers were being pressed so tightly together that it already seemed unlikely that the doors would be able to shut. A teenage boy with a wispy black moustache braced himself with both hands against the doorway, almost crushing a squat little woman in front of him, and only just succeeded in inching his backpack out of harm's way. The beeping doors closed and fell quiet. The tram jolted on its tracks, shaking the crushed passengers like teeth in a tin, and then it was on its way again, and Donna's eyes were carried away from the weeping woman's awful stare and then she was out of sight.

Her heart still pressing up against her throat, Donna took some deep breaths. It was too hot in the carriage now and she was getting damp under her armpits. She wanted to unbutton her coat and take her scarf off, but she didn't have the elbow room; any movement would collide with the salesman's crotch or the woman who had tutted, who was still giving her disapproving sideways glances. Instead, she opened her phone case again and texted Florrie: 'Can you talk? Important!'

That should bring her running, Donna thought. A good daughter ought to be concerned at that.

Florrie had never been quite normal, of course, in that regard, but Donna wasn't going to let her keep on shirking. They weren't best friends. They didn't go on lunch dates, and they were the wrong size to borrow each other's clothes. It infuriated Donna: all the ways in which Florrie resisted her mother's hopes.

'We're not that posh,' Josh had said when she was born. 'Who calls their baby *Florence* unless they've got a dishwasher and a 4x4?' Donna had persisted, though. And what had she gotten but ingratitude ever since?

She was far too hot now, and her head was swimming. She could feel the tension in her shoulders crawling up her neck. It wasn't fair, she thought. Of course, *she* was always the bad guy, of course Charlotte had made it sound like it was all Donna's fault.

'I've given her all the help I can,' Donna had said – she'd been firm on that, at least. 'I can't watch her all the time. I'm not a babysitter.'

That was when Charlotte had started bawling, making herself look plainer than ever under that ridiculous blue hair. What sort of colour was that for the workplace, anyway? Donna had never wanted to hire her in the first place, and she had made the presentation standards clear to her plenty of times. She'd taken her aside during her break even more times than Stinky Leo. *When you step inside this building, you represent the company.* But had she listened?

104

While Charlotte had been crying, Donna had noticed that she'd chewed the nails on her pudgy hands right down to the cuticle. They looked pink and raw like a child's, and made Donna want to shake her. She had suspected – for a long time now, probably since Donna's first day if she was being truly honest – that Charlotte was one of those women who went through life refusing to grow up.

'Perhaps your previous boss would have let you get away with this,' she'd had to say, about all the extra toilet trips, 'but I won't stand for it.'

That was the trouble with being an assertive person, sometimes. It didn't make you many friends.

The tram braked too hard at Firswood, and the tutting woman staggered against the man who chewed his beard. He barely looked up from the football on his phone and made no attempt to catch her. No text from Florrie, though Donna's message showed as 'read'.

A little jolt of adrenaline went through her – half exciting, half nasty, like a rollercoaster. She slowly lifted her arm, smelling herself faintly beneath her coat, and wiped the fug from the window once again, as the tram doors opened and those few unfortunates battled their way through the tangle of strangers' limbs to leave, before the would-be passengers surged forwards and trapped them there until Chorlton.

She was there. Impossible – completely impossible, but there stood the crying woman, inches away from Donna's window. Her wet coat and shoes, her shabby tote bag, her makeup congealing in the corners of her eyes. Donna was close enough to see more details now: her sagging, sobbing, purple mouth; the snot that glistened in the crevice of her upper lip.

She was looking at the tram doors. There were only three people in front of her and she was looking to see if there was space for her to board, and the rain and tears and snot were gathering and dripping from the end of her nose, and then she swung her eyes down to meet Donna's.

Her look then was so thick with hate, it felt like a slap. She crouched low, bringing that awful face level with Donna's and so close that if the window hadn't been between them she'd have felt her breath. And she *hissed*.

Then the doors of the flesh-stuffed tram beeped and beeped and closed again, and the ghoulish creature wasn't on it. Donna's blood was whooshing in her ears. There was no getting round it; people just didn't behave like that, they just did not go around hissing at strangers. Strangers they had never so much as spoken to and had no reason, no reason whatsoever to dislike. Donna's pulse was doing that fluttery thing again, she braved the annoyance of the tutting woman and opened her coat, but she couldn't get her scarf off. Besides, there was *absolutely no way* that the crying woman could have run from Trafford Bar to Firswood and made it there before the tram.

That only left one rational explanation. Perhaps she should've seen it coming, with all the stress she'd been under recently. She would tell HR on Monday, she decided. Look what this is doing to me! That stupid girl isn't the only one whose 'mental health' is suffering! If she could just keep her eyes closed until she reached her stop, perhaps she could keep this awful hallucination at bay. Donna felt better now she'd named it, but the fear was still horribly real.

'Who's being bullied now, Charlotte?' she would say on Monday – in front of lots of people, preferably. 'Are you satisfied, now you've driven me to the very edge of a breakdown?'

But it was Chorlton next, where the tram usually emptied out at least half of its passengers. If the crying woman was there again…

She couldn't wait for Florrie to text back; she'd have to call her. She dialled and pressed the phone hard against her ear.

'Mum? What's going on? I'm right in the middle of…' The tram horn blared and Donna didn't hear the rest, but it didn't matter. How many minutes before the next stop? How many had already passed?

'I'm on the tram!' she called clearly into the phone, keeping her voice bright and breezy for all the other passengers who were listening. 'I've had a difficult day, and I need you to -'

'Look Mum, can I call you later when you're home? I can hardly hear you, and I've got Sammy screaming his head off.' Donna fixed a smile on her face, but tears were building behind her eyes.

'Florrie, love, I need you to stay on the phone with me. I need to tell you that–'

'Sorry Mum, I'll call you tonight, okay?' She hung up.

Donna swallowed and said, 'Alright, darling! Speak later!' into the silence at the end of the phone, then removed it from her ear.

Was anybody looking at her? A tear fattened and threatened to spill from the corner of her eye, and she pressed it back in again with her finger. She glanced at the window, where a patch of greasy scenery still showed through the fog where she had rubbed it. She recognised those hedgerows, didn't she, because they were close to the next stop? How long now?

She jabbed at her phone screen, tears blurring her vision: 'CALL BACK NMOW'. But Florrie wouldn't. She wouldn't call this evening, either. Donna would have to chase and chase, and even then, her daughter would evade her, sticking the brats on to prattle at her, or putting her on speakerphone so Mark could listen. It was all part of the same monumental sulk – and over what? Because Donna hadn't made the right amount of fuss over the wedding, or the babies? Because she'd told a few home truths?

'People have it much worse than you,' she'd told Florrie when they'd last seen each other, four or five months back. 'You haven't even asked how my new job is going.'

The tram was slowing. A baby somewhere further down was screaming in its pushchair, making everyone wince. Its mother was singing to try and soothe it, her voice thin and self-conscious above the screech and rattle of the tram. Somewhere behind her, Donna could hear the tinny vibrations of pop music coming from someone else's headphones. The sound made her think of Charlotte, who left one ear bud in when Donna came to speak to her at her desk, and who often missed calls because she didn't hear her phone ring. Those things had been on Donna's list, but she was not even sure that Adele from HR had read the whole document.

The tram tooted its horn again, and jolted sickeningly to

a halt at Chorlton. Donna closed her eyes.

Around her, she felt the currents of pressure moving away from her towards the doors, and the cold damp air rushing in, and she heard the hostility in the muttered *Excuse me*s and *Can I get past you?*s as the salesman and the tutting woman and more passengers than she could count filed past her, and away. Should she go with them? But the hissing hallucination might follow her out into the open. And then she'd be soaked, and stranded, with no one official to call on it she were to faint, or…

No. She was safest where she was, and she just needed to get home. She needed a bath and a glass of wine. She needed Florrie to call her back, so Donna could tell her about all those awful things Charlotte had said about her, and the way Adele had sat there and let her and nodded like it wasn't all preposterous, like the list Donna had made wasn't reason enough to dismiss that lazy, attention-seeking lump of a girl, like Donna had been too critical, too angry, too overbearing. She needed Florrie so that she could take the sting out of it all by saying it aloud, so she could tell her it wasn't true, it wasn't, it wasn't.

The tram doors were closing. Donna couldn't tell if anyone new had got on; with her eyes squeezed shut, she could only feel that space had opened up around her. She wasn't sweltering in her layers anymore, and the sweat on her back and underneath her breasts felt cold. The tram creaked and moved off, and colourful shadows flickered across Donna's eyelids.

Was she here? The mother and baby must have got off, or else the child had just stopped crying. Was that awful woman close – sitting near her, perhaps, perhaps reaching out a hand?

Ridiculous. There were only three more stops to go; Donna could wait that long, surely. The need to look was building like an itch. She felt too naked, too vulnerable. How must she look? Were other people watching her, and smirking? Some of them had probably heard her phone call to Florrie, had probably noted the panic in her voice, had assumed she was unhinged. She opened her eyes.

The crying woman was standing at the other end of the carriage, but she wasn't crying anymore. Her eyes were fixed on Donna. The tram was still busier than she'd imagined and littered with standing passengers, but the spaces between them had yawned open. Donna shifted in her seat, so that a man in a red puffer jacket obscured the woman from her sight, and Donna from hers.

Deep breaths, slow breaths. Three stops to go, keep looking at the floor.

But she couldn't do it, and when she looked up again that ghastly figure was several paces closer, her stare still boring into Donna who thought,

She's going to kill me.

Donna stood up. She put her phone back in her pocket and tried to move towards the doors, getting stuck behind the man in the puffer jacket but that didn't matter, she just had to be ready to leave at the next stop. It was St Werburgh's Road, and she could walk from there, or get a taxi. She tried to hide how much her legs were shaking, and gripped the central yellow pole to keep herself upright. The passengers nearest to her shifted without looking at her, and again that face was closer, she was so close now that Donna knew there could be no escape, and her mouth fell open in a silent scream as the creature placed her small, pale hand just inches above hers, the fingers forming themselves into a grasp that was both childlike and lecherous, those eyes still burning burning burning.

The man in the red puffer jacket had moved aside to let her stand there, had relinquished his grip on the pole so she could hold it. *She was real.*

This close, Donna realised for the first time that there was something wrong, horribly wrong, with the *edges* of the crying woman. Her hairline, the skin around her eyes and mouth and fingernails. Had no one else around them noticed it? It was like her outer self was just a mask, and she could peel it off. Donna didn't want to look, but her eyes were drawn back to her over and over because she needed to know if she'd imagined it and she so desperately didn't want to see what might be underneath. Donna tried to stare at the floor, willing her to choose someone else, anyone else. Willing her to leave the tram and go after Charlotte, or Adele, or any of those cowards at work, or her neighbours, or Helen who had been her friend since nursery school, or her brother Michael.

She sank, slowly, haltingly down through the tangle of legs and damp coats and bags and umbrellas. The people around her tried not to see her: the weirdo sitting on their feet. They shuffled and rearranged themselves around her so a little dark cave opened up for her to hide in. The baby in its pram started to cry again and for a moment she felt the weight of Florrie in her arms, she saw her bright head flashing as she ran towards Donna in the playground. Then she felt the brush of cold flesh on her face and the words were coming out of Donna's mouth and she said: 'Take her, take Florrie. Take her instead.'

Ready or Not

When Misha lost her fifth baby tooth, she understood that she was going to die one day.

She couldn't say why it was this tooth in particular that had caused this revelation, but there it was, plain as the bloody molar in her palm: the truth, plucked out into the open from a place where it had been hiding, snug, and dark, and safe. To make way for something else that was, as yet, unknown, but coming – ready or not.

She was fond of this tooth. It had been loose in her mouth for what felt like forever, and she had dedicated many happy hours to it, unable to resist the urge to wiggle it with her tongue until her jaw ached and her mouth tasted like pennies.

'Stop it,' Misha's mother had said in the park, when she caught her staring fixedly into the distance, her mouth working with obscene concentration. 'You look strange. You don't want people to think you're strange, do you?'

Not being thought strange was very important in Misha's house. Her parents talked about it as if they believed they were under constant surveillance; it dictated the clothes Misha wore, and the time she went to bed, and the questions she was allowed to ask them, even in the car with the windows shut and the radio on. Sometimes, it made Misha feel like a celebrity; she simply could not be seen at the shopping centre in a pink jacket that clashed so horribly with her bright red Minnie Mouse t-shirt – she was far too important for that. But most of the time it made her feel afraid, and by the time her fifth tooth finally fell out, she had already learned the unspoken rule that meant she was always absent on school photograph day, and her mother made them walk the three miles home if a police car drove too slowly past their bus stop, and family holidays ended abruptly if they saw a man in a dark jacket more than once.

Her tooth came out one afternoon at school. Brown and gory, with its surprising root like a shark's tooth. She carried it home and presented it to her mum, who knew from looking at her that this was no time for the Tooth Fairy. Without a word, she took Misha upstairs to the master bedroom. She brought down a cardboard box that was hidden behind the hats and scarves in the top of their wardrobe. Misha watched, breathing shallowly, as her mother withdrew a little metal tin and opened it. Nestled inside, tucked up tenderly in a bed of tissue paper, were her other four baby teeth, to which Misha's mother now added this one – the biggest and lumpiest and best loved of them all. They looked like dead things, Misha thought. They looked private, and indecent, and like they shouldn't have been kept.

'There,' said Misha's mum. 'I'll keep them nice and safe.'

Misha looked at what else was in the shoebox. If she had been hoping for baby photos – which the other children sometimes brought in for 'Show and Tell', she was disappointed. Instead, there were some shells she remembered collecting from the beach at Formby, and a purple bow that had been cut from her favourite dress when she'd outgrown it, and some drawings she'd made of the house they used to live in and had been so sad to leave. And there, underneath, in another little tissue paper parcel, was a

114

lock of hair; silky and fair and utterly unlike Misha's.

'That was your father's baby hair,' said Misha's mum, and took it from her.

There were lots of things that Misha wanted to ask. But the unspoken rule told her that she would only be allowed one question, and so she prioritised, and said, 'What will happen to my teeth after I die?'.

Until the words were out of her mouth, Misha didn't realise that she had been hoping for a comforting lie. Another mother, she thought, might have hugged her and said, 'You're never going to die, sweetheart. Don't worry. Your dad and I will look after you.' But hers didn't. She put away the shoebox, carefully tucking it in behind the scarves and sliding back the wardrobe door.

Then she looked at Misha, and said, 'I suppose they'll stay here. Unless somebody finds them, and takes them away.'

A few weeks later, Misha was allowed to host her first ever birthday party. Perhaps her parents felt she needed cheering up; or maybe it was just the least strange thing and had to be done, given that her class teacher had expressed concern about Misha's newfound obsession with how soon various people and animals were going to die, and what would happen to their bodies.

They were about to start a game of pass-the-parcel, when Misha found herself caught up in a conversation about babyhood. Her friend Sapphire had been a huge baby, Sapphire's mum was saying – nine and a half pounds! – which made Sapphire grin like it was a great achievement on her part, and the grown-up women exchange knowing grimaces.

'How much did you weigh when you were born, Misha – do you know?' asked Sapphire's mum, and Misha shook her head, suddenly ashamed.

'Mum says I was a very happy baby,' she said, to appease her audience. 'The first time I looked at her I smiled, and that's how she knew that I was hers to keep.'

The atmosphere in the room changed then. Misha knew that she had broken the rules, and when she saw her dad's face she was afraid that he was going to stop the party and send everyone home.

'Come on then, let's get on with the game!' he said, too loudly. He stopped the music so that everybody got a present except Misha, which the other parents chose politely not to notice. Inside, Misha felt something wobbling, and when she swallowed there was a lump in her throat that hurt her. She worried that she had lost another tooth without realising, and got it lodged there. When it was time to blow out the candles on her cake, she wished that she was dead already, and buried somewhere quietly in the ground, where she could stay very still, and no one would watch her for mistakes.

At school they started watching her, too. Misha stayed inside at playtime and drew pictures. All smiley, happy families: Mum, Dad, Misha. Mum, Dad, Misha. Once, she forgot to draw Dad's glasses, and had to race back during dinner break to ask to put it right.

'I just forgot,' she mumbled to her teacher, bending low over the page and pressing as hard as she could with the pencil. His frames were black, but all the crayons had been packed away. Mrs Lingley looked up a number on her phone and called it.

The day before they moved again, Misha waited until her parents were outside loading up the van, and climbed up on her mum's sewing chest to retrieve the shoe box. Underneath more tissue paper and the lock of hair, she found a photograph of some other children playing, taken from a distance, and a map with places circled on it, but these she discarded. She took her five teeth from the little tin and carried them out into the garden, where she buried them. She told herself a story in which they would grow, like trees, into other children; into brothers and sisters who would have hair and eyes like hers, and who she would be reunited with one day. But really, she just wanted to leave a piece of herself behind in this place that had been her home; perhaps to be dug up by some future archaeologist, when she herself was long gone.

'You are a very special girl,' said her mum, squeezing her leg from the front seat as they drove away, the streetlights burning like birthday candles as they flashed past them in the dark. Misha wondered if she meant 'different', which was bad, or 'precious', which was good, but she didn't ask.

In another town, she would grow into a woman who holds onto things too tightly, who would frighten people with the sort of longing it is difficult to disguise, whose friends would talk about 'needing a break from'. But for now, she was seven years old, and still the age when adults think your wounds are soon forgotten if you cease to mention them. The space in her mouth would not be empty for long; already she could feel a sharp point emerging, and she imagined she was a snake shedding its skin, the new,

117

grown up Misha rising from where it has always been; waiting, inside herself. Coming. Ready or not.

A conversation recorded before the end of the experiment

First, we feel we ought to recognise that the adjustment period has been difficult for both sides. We knew there would be challenges and we prepared for those as best we could, but there have also been difficulties we did not foresee. And we acknowledge that there were no plans in place where in hindsight we ought to have anticipated certain... eventualities. And this has caused suffering for all concerned.

Hind. Sight.

Yes. A wonderful thing, as they say.

What is—?

Oh, of course. My apologies. Hindsight. To, um— to look back, behind you, at the path that has brought you to this point. If we'd known then what we know now. We would have done things differently.

To look behind you.

Yes.

**To look back.
At your hind legs?**

Well.
I suppose so.
In a manner of speaking.

Okay.

Okay?

Nodding. We are nodding. That we hear

> **and understand what you are saying though
> not necessarily that we agree. Yes?**

Yes?

> **That is the correct way to mean the nodding?**

It's—yes, it's a start. That we are listening
and understanding each other—that's an
important start. I think we can agree on that!

> **We are nodding.**

Okay, then.

So.

One of the things I think I should explain is that
it was a shock to most of us when we arrived and
saw you for the first time. In the flesh, as it were.
You see, there was propaganda back home.
We'd been told you were not so different from us.
And of course that's true in some ways, we do
have plenty in common. But you see, at first sight...
They'd used the word—it's offensive, I know, I see
that now—but the messaging back home used the
word *humanoid*, and that led us to think...

> **You thought we would be having legs.**

It...

It surprised us that you didn't. That you don't.
Among... other things.
It was just a bit of a shock, really, and I think that—
that shock—it frightened some of us, and that's why
some of us didn't behave as we, *they*, ought to have done.
But then of course—and I'm not making excuses for those
initial settlers here—we must remember that this is the
very first time two parties have tried to share a

clean world. There were bound to be teething problems.

That we do not agree.

Our teeth are not a problem.

Well. Not for you, perhaps. But for us—

Our teeth are not a problem.

It's...

It's an expression. It's an idiom, which...

which... complicates things, I realise.

I'm sorry.

I mean simply to say that there were bound to be

some problems. To begin with.

Bound to be.

Inevitably.

To be.

Bound?

Well...

Look.

Perhaps—perhaps we—perhaps that's where

we should begin.

To be bound.

Boundaries. The bounds. Our territories,

and the marking of borders.

It will not help, this marking.

We think it might. If boundaries are to

be enforced—

How is it you would enforce
boundaries against us?

Enforce?

You said:
En.

121

Force.

Oh. I see.
I see the misunderstanding.
Look.
We're not talking about anything involving
actual physical force. Quite the opposite, in fact.
Boundaries can be maintained simply by mutual
agreement.

Enforced without.

Without what?

Force.

Quite. Well, yes. Exactly.
The point is. What we want—what we all
want, surely—is to keep our two *peoples*
peacefully apart. We think that should be
perfectly possible. All we need is your
co-operation.

Co-operation.
Meaning?
Collective. Operation.
Yes?

Exactly that.

This we cannot do.

I...
Might I ask why not?

One world we are sharing. Only one.
What will you do with your borders?
Cut this world and make two?
It is not possible.
We read that where you come from

                              there are piece-lands.

Peace-lands?

                    Small pieces of land, separated by sea.

Oh! Islands.

                                   Yes, yes. Eye-lands.
                         Because you see them but you cannot
                              reach them without a plan—yes?
                          These eye-lands. We do not have these.
                          What you sow over there will change the
                             grazing of the livestock we keep here.
                                   It is like a man. It is like you.
                                   If I tear you, you will die.

That's true, but—but we're not suggesting
any—anything like that. It's just a question of
differentiating where we can go and where
you can go. There is a method, I'm told, of
harmlessly changing the colour of soil so that
everyone knows: if I'm on red soil, that's fine;
I am safe and I'm allowed to be here. But if I
look down and I see that the soil is blue...

                                   What is this colour?

I'm sorry?
I thought you could...
They told us you could see in colour.

                                   We can see so.
                            We understand a woman when
                         she says: *most plants are green.*
                           We have seen this green, but it is
                                   not one thing.
                            One plant has many parts.

123

> They are all themselves.
> Yet this woman says: *all of this is green.*
> So we ask her: what is green?

I see.

> And so, to you, we ask: what is blue?
> The soil is made from millions of
> fragments, and they are all themselves.
> How can they all be blue?

I see.
Yes, I see.
You know, this is exactly why we need a dialogue.
We've just learnt something there, about you, that
we never would've thought of on our own.
The soil idea—that's no good then. So what?
We'll throw it out. We'll throw out as many ideas
as we need to, and when we find the right one, it
will be based on mutual understanding and respect.

> *Ressspect.*
> We have not heard this before.

Well, it means...
To believe that another party is important.
That they are—at least—equal to oneself.
To treat them with dignity.

> Your blue soil.
> This would give you dignity?

As I say, it doesn't have to be the soil.

> But your soils would show
> that you and we are equal.

Yes. That's really central, actually. That's what
it all comes down to at the end of the day. To

124

be friends, we must be equals.

                      We see.
       But why only when it is dark?

I'm sorry?

       You would like us to be equal
       only at the end of the day?

No, no. I don't mean...
It's an idiom.

       Do you mean only for this day,
   or is it for all days that you are speaking?

It's just an expression.

       Yes. We are laughing.

Oh?
I can't hear—

            Inside.
       Inside ourselves, we are doing
       what we think you call laughing.

Oh.
Why?

          We are amused.
       We are teasing you with these
       questions about the end of the day.

Ah, okay. That's fine.
A bit of levity. That's fine.

       But also we laugh because
       we cannot think you equal to us.

Excuse me?
What do you mean by that, exactly?

       You may think that we are
       equal friends. You may give us your

125

dignite—your dignutt—

Dignity.

Dignity.
But we cannot.

Well, then.
I think we've arrived at another of these
examples. It's our language barrier interfering
again. Or it's our cultural differences showing!
You see, if I didn't know better, I could take
offence at what you just said.
It sounded like you were saying you
think we're beneath you. Our species.

Yes.
These are the sounds we mean to make.

Oh. I see.
Perhaps...
Perhaps this is a subject we can come back to,
after we've given more thought to the practicalities.
I have a list here. Points to discuss. Agenda items.
Let me see...
Food supplies?
We're all concerned about food, aren't we?

We are not so concerned.

But it's an issue, isn't it? It's a problem.
Neither of us seems to have anticipated
quite how quickly certain shortages would
emerge. And we did think we had agreed—
I mean, it's in the initial settlement contract,
isn't it? The terms for dividing and managing
the food supply. If you'd care to have another

126

look at the document—

This is not necessary.

No, please. Be my guest. I insist.
Jenny?
Jenny here—Jenny? Don't be silly, it's fine.
Jenny is going to pass it through the secure
window for you.
That's it.

We have read this previously.

If you'd care to look—clause four, right there.
You'll see it was agreed that both sides would
commit to a plant-based diet until livestock
imports had reached a level sufficient to
allow the establishment of sustainable populations.

We have read this.

Can you explain to me, then, why your side
felt you couldn't abide by that agreement?

It is not good, this translation here.

It was discussed at great length,
before it was agreed. Wasn't it?
I mean—
What are you saying, exactly?
That part of the settlement contract wasn't
properly understood by your leadership?

**It is understood. But it is very badly
phrased. Who did this?**

I don't think I have a name to give you just now.
It was all done very officially, though.
I can assure you of that.
Are you saying you would like a new translation?

127

No.

So, then?

Yes?

Can you explain to me why you, your *people*,
felt it impossible to abide by the agreement?
For instance—and I realise it might be
controversial to bring this up but I
really think it's the elephant in the—
Never mind. Ignore that.
My question to you is: What happened to the
people on board the 917?

This was unfortunate.

Yes. It was.
There are all sorts of rumours that we have not
exactly managed to contain. I would never have
believed them but I saw the drone footage, and...
Well, I was frightened. A lot of people
found it very frightening because it just doesn't
seem to make any sense.
Can you explain it to me?

We were very hungry.

You must see—
Jenny, no. It's all right. It's all right.
Look.
You must see why we don't feel that that,
your *hunger*,
justifies your actions.

We do not know what you feel.
We have our own feelings.

Well, look. Tell me this, at least.

Why did our new arrivals behave the way they did
when they came into contact with you? Was
something said? Were threats made?
Were they poisoned or was there—did you
release some sort of inhalant to make them
suggestible or, or immune to pain? To rob
them of their wits?

We did not do any of these things.

Then what?
This is very—
Wait.
What is that? I'm hearing—
Is that—
What I'm hearing now, is *that* laughter?

Our laughter is no longer inside us.

You're laughing at me?

At your people.

My people?

We remember them.

The ones you took.

We remember them.

Do you?
I remember. Watching them arrive.
After waiting for their arrival for so long.
Seeing that crowd of you there, encircling them.
Do you know how traumatic that was?
They knew what had been happening—they knew
what it meant, as soon as they saw you.
But they walked towards you as calm,
as placid, as docile as—

Yes?

I can't say it.

Your language is deficient, then.

There was a man I used to work with.
I saw him dismembered and devoured.
His arm was ripped off and fed to one of
your offspring. He didn't even flinch.
He just waited for you to come back for
the rest of him. I saw a woman unbutton her
uniform to expose her torso. Then she just
stood there as she was sliced open, navel
to sternum, and had her organs extracted.

They were consumed.

But how did you do it?

It is not possible to say.

So, then, how do we broker peace?
How do we find a way forward if we can't be
sure that it won't happen again? If we don't
even know what weapon it is you have at your
disposal that can do something like that, let
alone get you to surrender it? How do we—
how do we do it if we can't get an assurance
that this atrocity was just, you know, just a
skirmish, a misunderstanding? Part of the
teething problems. Do you understand my
dilemma? *Our* dilemma?

We understand it.

And are you *nodding*?

We do not know.
If we can help you.

                In the way you want.
We need an answer. You see that, don't you?
Today, between us—we have the power to
deliver reassurances.
For instance—
What about our settlement?
Can we talk about New Copenhagen?

                This *new* confuses us.
           We have never seen this first Copenhagen.
            This one is for us the first Copenhagen.
Are you teasing me again?
Do you call it something else?

          We do not call it. It is not a dog, which you
            teach a sound to make it come to you, as
                I have seen in your archives.
                    We are not like you.
          We do not name a thing because we have
            seen it. Our words are not instruments
                    of ownership.
Yes, yes. All right. Shall we stick to our name
for the place, then, if your people haven't
given it one? We might struggle to make
progress if we can't even refer to places.

         If we did refer to it, you would not be able
                    to pronounce.
Well, *all right* then.
New Copenhagen—as we call it.
We'd like to clarify whether
your actions there have been in order to
claim that particular territory?

131

To take it from us?
We thought—
I thought—
Some of us thought you meant for your
hostility to be taken as a show of strength,
that's all. A play for dominance.

                                                  We are nodding.

Nodding at what?

                                                  At your words.

Which words? Which bit?

                                  The words that say we
                              meant to show you our dominance.

I'm right? You're confirming this?

                            We do not need to show what is a fact.

And—
Oh, God.
And this is the official line?
If this is the official line, then—
New Copenhagen, what happened there
last week.
Is an act of warfare.

                                              Warfare.

Warfare.

                                              War.
                                              Fare.
                                As in: to pay?
                                      A toll?

I really don't have a clue about the etymology
of that word. And frankly, I think it's
distracting us from what's really important here.

The lives of each of our peoples are depending on
the outcome of this conversation. They're the
important things for us to focus on.

> **Important?**
> **This is not the word we use.**

Perhaps—

> *Interesting.*
> **This is the word we use.**
> **Your lives are *interesting* to us.**
> **Not important.**

And this is—again—this is the official line?
You're speaking on behalf of the leadership?
Can you tell me... I hope I'm not being impertinent
when I ask this, but—what's your role? I mean,
where are you in the hierarchy? What
level of expertise do you have, to negotiate
our future cohabitation?

> **It is difficult. To translate.**

Try me.

> **I am one who—**
> **how is it said by you?—**
> *accumulates.*

Accumulates what?

> **Knowledge.**

Knowledge of?

> **Life.**
> **The life of the world.**

I don't understand.

> **Life. *Forms.***
> **You say: *I study*. Life forms.**

                              Other than ourselves.

You mean—
You're a student?

                    I wish to accumulate knowledge
                                      of your people.

You're just a student.

                    While the opportunity remains open.
                    While you remain here in sufficient
                                             numbers.

Oh, God.

                                        Oh. God?

What have we done?

                    Are we intended to answer this question?
What have we done? What have we—?

                         Your words are continuing but
                         they are not moving forward.

What have we done? Oh, God, what have—
what can we—what are we supposed to—
Oh, God. A fucking *student?*

                    This *fucking*—this you are using for emphasis?
                                      I did not know.

               Your species: I find it very *fucking* interesting.
Help me. Oh, God.
Help us all.

                    Do you wish for us to end our talking now?

Can you—
Okay.
Just give me a minute.
Okay. All right.
You have to understand.

                                    134

I had hoped...
No, that doesn't matter.
They sent you. A student. This wasn't
easy to arrange. And they sent *you*.
But can you—
You can at least take a message back,
can't you? You can go back to the leadership
and tell them, from me, tell them...

If you wish it.

I do. I do wish it. Very much.
Tell them...
Look, I'm sorry. I'm sorry I got upset just now.
These are difficult times. I just—I'm sure...
I'm sure they are difficult on your side too.
I want you to tell them we'd still like to
work towards partnership. Collaboration.

Co-operation.

Yes. Yes, that's right.
We don't want a war.

No. You do not.

We only want to set some boundaries, you see?
You mustn't think of them as anything but
the foundations of a friendship.
Take this window between us now, for instance.
It doesn't only separate us. It allows us to sit
face-to-face. It has made this conversation possible.

This is the message we should convey?

Yes. Yes, but listen. Understand it first.
All right?
Look at this glass. Look at what it does.

135

Look at what it *allows* us to do in one
another's company.
You are there and I am here and we can talk like
equals because we both know we are safe.
And it will take time, of course, to build walls
this strong, if that's what's needed,
across our territories, however we
agree to map them out. But when we come
to a clean world we are rich in time. We can
start small, and we can slowly expand our boundaries
until our respective peoples have their own protected
spaces in which to live. And even if it is the work
of many generations, well, what does it matter?
Just think what we might accomplish next,
after all those lifetimes of working together!

         We understand your message.

Tell them—
Tell them that our ability to apply ourselves
to a common goal will bring my people and your
people as close as any neighbours could hope
to be. It will be just like this, all the world over.

              Very good.

A whole world that works just like this room.
Borders between our territories, fixed
but crystal clear, functioning exactly like this pane
of glass, through which we can talk, and trade,
and share ideas.

      This glass: you must take it down now.

What?
Oh, yes.

I must.

The button is there, by your wrist.

Yes.
I see.
Thank you.

The Savage Chapel

The church is big today. If you approach Macclesfield's St Michael and All Angel's from the south side, you wouldn't know the difference, but from Church Street you can't avoid the three levels of glass and steel. Enter, and you can see how the new enlarged nave sprawls itself like the fat belly of an old vicar, its dark stone lifting your eyes and heart to heaven.

I am glad it is not a building day, but I find it disconcerting, all this chopping and changing, old to new and back again. I would like to go and rest inside the Legh chapel, but today it is full of too-bright furnishings and books for children, and I want a more sombre atmosphere in which to wait for him.

My own chapel is named for me, of course: the Savage Chapel. It is my starting and my end point; the centre from which I may wander, though not far, like a tethered dog. If I stray and find myself unravelling, it is here that I come back to: encased, entombed. Safe as only the dead are safe.

My name, Thomas Savage, was perhaps an odd one for a priest, but I always liked it. It is particularly fitting for this chapel, which is, on most days, used for quiet contemplation and for prayer. Those things sound gentle, but the people who come to sit here are the carriers of all sorts of violent feeling. We tend to forget that the heart is a muscle. These days I see a great deal of sentiment for the mild-mannered Christ, but personally I always preferred him in a rage, throwing the merchants from the temple.

Have I introduced you to our priest yet? If I haven't, I

blame my condition; memory is not my strong point anymore. His foot has just struck the fourth of the 108 steps. It has been raining, and he is watching his shoes just now, but by the fifty-second step he will look up and see the flank of the church, the stained glass lying flat and grey, luminous only from the inside.

There is a saying now that I do not like: *Home is where the heart is.* It's the sort of trite thing that women in the congregation embroider onto cushions and little lavender bags. Sometimes they decorate them with hearts as a child might draw them, two humps like breasts or buttocks, meeting in a point. They do not depict me, of course. Not the fist of flesh that they interred here, plucked from my body before it was laid to rest at York Minster, as was an archbishop's proper right. I do not know if the remainder of my spirit – the spirit of my lungs, my legs, my pronounced and hefty intellect – rises and stalks that great church, or squeezes itself onto pews and murmurs into the ears of the mourners, the confessors, the hypocrites. I often wonder what the nature of that ghost might be. Divorced, as it is, from me – as later the boy who watched me marry Catherine of Aragon to his brother would divorce himself from her and from the holy see of Rome, leaving his people to scratch across the arid landscape of Protestantism, far from the incense and the awe of the one true faith. What the Lutherans never understood is that ordinary people prefer magic to symbolism. Who wants to eat a wafer that is only a wafer, if last week you were offered the actual meat of God?

I always gave a good sermon, and I preached to kings.

139

But perhaps, without me, my ghost is not even a Catholic.

I beg your pardon, though. I lose my focus easily. Our friend is on the ninety-ninth step. He keeps a leather bag tucked in tight against himself to save it from the rain; it is older than it looks, he is that sort of person. I shoo away the quiet ones who are cluttering up the place with their contemplations, and most of them sense my hostility and shuffle out. One who stays is a woman who is weeping softly. She lights a candle; it burns down in the flicker of a pulse and extinguishes. She lights another, and splits herself, and lights another, until there are fifty of her, days and months and years of her, folding over each other and spreading out like a fan, all their little lights flickering in and out of existence. One of her older selves bends to write a prayer request. *Please pray for my son. He is lost.*

I take a deep breath. I used to be able to control this sort of thing with a bit of concentration, but it is getting worse. For the heart, it seems, time does not move forwards and backwards, but happens all at once. To the heart everything is present tense.

Our man comes in, and brings the evening with him. He both believes he is alone and knows he cannot be, and he mutters something; a prayer, I suppose, from that silly little English book he carries. Over the years, I have sometimes lifted it from his pocket while he sleeps and been amused by its practical content: *For Fair Weather, In the Time of Plague or Sickness, For Peace and Deliverence from our Enemies.* He is too beautiful, really, to be a schoolteacher or a priest. It is distracting to have him around the place, with his pale eyes and his neat, clean hands. I try to make myself visible to him and think myself his equal in height, if a little broader. At one time, I could make myself as solid as a man and twice as tall, or I could manifest as an altar, or an organ pipe, or a communion cup. It was a relief, I'll admit, to find my heart was not devoid of humour, but perhaps my other ghost is very serious indeed. One reckless evening, I hid myself inside a statue of the Virgin Mary, and the older members of the congregation who still remembered their rosary beads and their saints' relics dipped their heads and washed my feet in tears.

But, alas. Now I can only hover at the edges of his vision, casting no shadow, obscuring nothing that might lie behind me. I do my best, and I put myself between him and the little priest-door beyond which he lives.

'Brother,' I say, and I confess that my tone is not only brotherly. I must stand close to make him hear me, and he jumps. The rain has made his hair look darker than it is, and he smells of it; yes, of musk, and of rain. For a moment there are forty of him, very young and just arrived, or pulling on his gown, or sitting close to the father of a troubled boy. But then he is one man again, and his expression is unhappy.

We sit together on the bench that has become our meeting place. I can feel that the bag he rests between us is heavy, and so he has brought the instruments I asked him to. It is the same bag from which he has drawn papers criss-crossed with his own dense handwriting: his notes on others like me, from whom we hoped, before my condition worsened that we might learn something. Some were names that I knew well. Richard the Lionheart, named for what he was supposed to have eaten, had his own heart preserved in a casket and taken to the cathedral in Rouen. Henry I, who met his unenviable end by eating poisoned eels, had his heart sewn into the hide of a bull to be transported home. And there were other names I did not know. *Thomas Hardy. Frederic Chopin.* He told me that a man called Byron plucked the flaming heart from his friend Shelley's body as it burned on a beach and gave it to his wife, who wrote a book about how men are monstrous.

There are no women on his list, presumably because they have mostly lacked the import to be needed in two places at once. I told him once that I felt a woman would be better suited to this heart-ghost existence, given as they are in life to being ruled by their emotions. One of the stained glass graces – Charity, I think it was – laughed in my face when she heard that, and her sisters had to shake her.

It was quite the thesis, really, that he wrote for me. But my fading out, my increasingly garbled state of mind... For these things, he has discovered no cure.

He twists his hands together. He does not want to do what I have brought him here for, and he looks around the room, at his sheets of research, at anything but me. But has he managed to discover, I ask him, dripping wax on him with one of the weeping women's candles to reclaim his full attention, whether any of these famous hearts has formed a ghost like mine? And, being formed, if they have suffered the same predicament: this timelessness, this changing and merging of centuries, this experiential affliction that is separating cause from its effect and making the very bonds of me loosen and fade?

He shakes his head. Around us, the little statues of my

great nephew's children torment me, switching themselves from flesh to stone and back again. The Breeches Bible in the corner clothes and unclothes Adam and Eve. In the church behind us, they hold a funeral for the weeping woman's son, who has been found at last. She does not see or hear it, but remains in the Savage Chapel, gilding us with the glow of hundreds of candles, all her backs turned to her son's casket as it is carried up the aisle by strangers. The roof above me builds and rebuilds itself, letting the weather in.

'Please,' I ask him.

He takes a hammer and chisel from his bag and cuts me from the wall. I direct him to the exact place, but the stone does not give me up easily. The noise of the hammer striking metal sets off a cacophony of complaint from every statue between the Pardon Brass and the pulpit, and sweat further dampens the hair at his temples; dust settles on the sleeves of his coat. My urn is small and I feel the tug of it, as he lifts me out and holds me in his hands. I never lay with another man while I had a body, but at this touch he makes me sorry for it. He gazes at me, at the faintest thickening of the air beside him.

He would do it if I asked him. He would carry me to York and rest me flat against the earth that covers me, and in that churchyard my spirit would be whole again. I would be reunited with my reasonable mind, with my skull and my belly and my cock. There have been many nights when we have whispered to each other, and he has unburdened himself to the ghost in the wall as he never has in confession. There was a man he loved, but spurned, as the penitent sinner that his faith would have him be. He is

143

haunted by that love, although he is innocent of his future, which I wish I did not know. To the heart, everything is present tense. But I am a coward, and I do not tell him that we stand in the light of his mother's candles. That our weeping woman weeps for him, her prayer requests aging and curling up like leaves. That his pain, at last, will lead him to do a thing beyond the Lord's forgiveness, and to be found in a cold place far from those who cherished him. For him, the funeral behind us is still very far away. It is moving closer, but there are years between them.

He holds me still, his little comfort in his warm hands.

'Never mind,' I say, and I press my weightlessness against his chest until he understands me. He holds me on his lap, and there we are the only things that do not tremble.

There cannot be long now. If my better spirit is in York, then let it lie there. If we were reunited, it would once again subsume me, and I would, perhaps, forget these hundreds of years of exile; so many of them spent watching or waiting for this man as he kneels, hands clasped, baring his soul, or brings the boys from the King's School to mass, or comforts the grieving and the helpless from whom I cannot seem to look away. I would forget (I know I would, for I was ever practical) the way he bends his head to pray, his smiling lips, the narrow breadth of his shoulders. I would present him to St Peter at the gates to paradise as one more thing that I have sacrificed for the eternity of my soul. He would be weighed on golden scales against my virtues; a lonely sin accrued after the bread and ale was passed over my cooling body and swallowed by a sin-eater, who knew not what he took into himself, but only hoped that he was paid its weight in gold.

We wait a while. This is a sermon, too. All that I am, I give unto my God. Every moment, I can feel myself dissolving into air.

Acknowledgements

This is my first book, so there are far too many people to thank.

Straight off, I must say thank you to my wonderful publisher Farhana Shaikh. I first came to know Farhana through working on her 'A Brief Pause' workshop series during lockdown, and it was only about five minutes into our first conversation that I knew this was somebody I wanted to work with and would follow into almost any creative project. It's been a dream come true to publish this collection with you, and I couldn't have asked for a better home for my stories than Dahlia Books.

I also owe this collection in huge part to my wonderful fellow writer friends, and to the wider Manchester literature scene which has nurtured me so well for over a decade. In particular, I want to thank my 'Gaslamp' writers' group: Dave Hartley (without whose invitation, encouragement, and example I don't think I'd have written any of these stories at all), Tom Mason (for the early Zoom writing mornings), Benjamin Judge (who solved the title story of this collection), Fat Roland, Rob Cutforth, Dan Carpenter, Nici West, and Beth Underdown (who has shared so generously in the nitty-gritty of MANY writing projects). Thank you also to Polly Checkland-Harding, whose patience, insight and curiosity know no limits; Rosie Garland, for being the most nourishing formal and informal mentor I could have asked for. Big thanks to my fellow Manchester literature event organisers for their camaraderie and for commissioning several of the stories that made it into this book, particularly David Gaffney, Joe Daly, Fat Roland (again), Kate Feld, Jack Nicholls, Jazz Chatfield, Adam Farrer, Nija Dalal-Small, Sarah-Clare Conlon, and my First Draft team, Harry Jelley and Andrew Williamson. Thank you also to Tania Hershman, whose friendship has inspired and motivated me so much.

Thank you to my mum, whose handwriting I traced when she taught me write my very first stories. She keeps a shelf in her house for my published work, and the thought of that shelf has buoyed me up through many a dark rejection day. To Fiona Davidson, for the book chats and for cheering me on. Also to my dad, for the theatre trips and for pushing me towards writing when I couldn't see past wanting to be an actor; and to Esteban and Bonnie, for their love and support through all our darkest times. And thank you to Amy McLaughlin, who never fails to celebrate my wins, and who has never once let me get away with a wanky Instagram post.

Finally, and most importantly, thank you to my wife Rachel Fernández-Arias, to whom this book is dedicated. Collectively, these stories have taken me ten years to write, and during that time you have been my best and most devoted cheerleader. You have sat through so many literature nights in sweaty pubs, softened so many disappointments, and celebrated so many victories. It's no small challenge, being married to someone who has chosen such a rollercoaster of a career; and yet whenever I write something new and ask if you want to read it, you only ever say 'Yes please'. Thank you, thank you.

About the Author

Abi Hynes is an award-winning drama and fiction writer based in Manchester. Her short stories have been published widely in print and online, including in Black Static and Interzone, and in short fiction anthologies from Boudicca Press, Fairlight Books and Splice. She won the Cambridge Short Story Prize in 2020 and was shortlisted for the Bath Flash Fiction 'Novella in Flash' Award in 2017.

Her plays have been performed across the UK, and she has written four episodes of historical audio drama DARK HARBOUR. She also writes for TV, and her script LONG LOST was on the Brit List in 2022.